Nina flipped through the photos taken at the crime scene and stopped when she noticed one of herself and Wyatt, the two of them so focused on each other they hadn't even noticed a flash going off.

They were standing together, Wyatt's expression was hot, even passionate, and his posture was open, powerful, protective. She was leaning toward him, her neck slightly arched, as if opening herself to his kiss.

Needing a distraction, she turned to Wyatt and said, "Take me to the lab."

"No, it's too late. Besides, you're exhausted. I need to take you upstairs and put you to bed."

He looked at her, his blue eyes twinkling, and a hot thrill coursed through her at the idea of him lifting her in his arms and carrying her upstairs. She swallowed, and the twinkle in his eyes faded, replaced by an intensity she hadn't seen before. He looked like…

He looked like he did in the photo. Hot, powerful, passionate.

Something started to burn deep inside her. She lifted her chin just slightly and they stared at each other. Then Wyatt blinked, breaking the moment.

But not before some silent promise was made.

MALLORY KANE

CLASSIFIED COWBOY

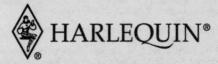

TORONTO • NEW YORK • LONDON
AMSTERDAM • PARIS • SYDNEY • HAMBURG
STOCKHOLM • ATHENS • TOKYO • MILAN • MADRID
PRAGUE • WARSAW • BUDAPEST • AUCKLAND

For my Daddy, who loves reading my books.

Recycling programs
for this product may
not exist in your area.

ISBN-13: 978-0-373-69447-1

CLASSIFIED COWBOY

Copyright © 2010 by Rickey R. Mallory

www.eHarlequin.com

Printed in U.S.A.

ABOUT THE AUTHOR

Mallory Kane credits her love of books to her mother, a librarian, who taught her that books are a precious resource and should be treated with loving respect. Her father and grandfather were steeped in the Southern tradition of oral history and could hold an audience spellbound for hours with their storytelling skills. Mallory aspires to be as good a storyteller as her father.

Mallory lives in Mississippi with her computer-genius husband, their two fascinating cats and, at current count, seven computers. She loves to hear from readers. You can write her at mallory@mallorykane.com or via Harlequin Books.

Books by Mallory Kane

HARLEQUIN INTRIGUE

927—COVERT MAKEOVER
965—SIX-GUN INVESTIGATION
992—JUROR NO. 7
1021—A FATHER'S SACRIFICE
1037—SILENT GUARDIAN
1069—THE HEART OF BRODY McQUADE
1086—SOLVING THE MYSTERIOUS STRANGER
1103—HIGH SCHOOL REUNION
1158—HIS BEST FRIEND'S BABY†
1162—THE SHARPSHOOTER'S SECRET SON†
1168—THE COLONEL'S WIDOW?†
1180—CLASSIFIED COWBOY

†Black Hills Brotherhood

CAST OF CHARACTERS

Lt. Wyatt Colter—A lieutenant in the Special Investigations Unit of the Texas Rangers, he was assigned to protect Marcie James, but she was kidnapped on his watch. Now he's obsessed with solving the mystery of her disappearance.

Nina Jacobson—This beautiful forensic anthropologist pulled strings to get assigned to investigate the mysterious bones uncovered in Comanche Creek. She's not about to let Wyatt out of her sight until the mystery is solved.

Marcie James—On the eve of testifying in a shady land deal, the mayor's assistant went missing and hasn't been heard from in two years. Was her disappearance by choice or against her will?

Daniel Taabe—Did this leader of the Native American community in Comanche Creek steal bones from the crime scene?

Woodrow "Woody" Sadler—The mayor seems cooperative, but could he have greased the way for Jonah Becker's fraudulent land deal?

Deputy Shane Tolbert—Did his stormy relationship with Marcie James indicate a violent nature?

Trace Becker—Jonah Becker's ruthless son would do anything to protect his daddy's money.

Billy Whitley—How far would he go to cover up his illegal dealings?

Charla Whitley—Charla's position with the mayor's office could have come in handy when her husband, Billy, needed her help.

Jerry Collier—Marcie's former boss almost came to blows with Daniel Taabe and was heard threatening Marcie.

Jeff Marquez—As an EMT at a teaching medical center, he was in the perfect position to help Marcie fake her kidnapping and death.

Chapter One

"Hey! What the hell are you doing?" Texas Ranger Lieutenant Wyatt Colter slammed the door of his Jeep Liberty and crossed the limestone road in three long, crunching strides.

It had taken him longer than he'd intended to get here. Jonah Becker's spread was huge—as big as Comanche Creek, Texas, was small. Becker had twelve thousand acres. The entire city limits of Comanche Creek would fit in the southeast corner of the spread.

Right now, though, Wyatt was much more concerned with the northwest corner, where human bones had been unearthed by the road crew, which Becker had fought so hard to keep off his land.

This small piece of real estate was Wyatt's crime scene, and the owners of the two mud-spattered SUVs had breached it. Where in hell was the deputy assigned to guard the scene?

Just as he drew in breath to yell again, the growl of a generator cut through the damp night air. A large spotlight snapped on with an almost audible whoosh. He headed toward it.

"Ben, hit your light!" a kid yelled. His long-billed

baseball cap sat askew on his head, and his pants looked as if they were going to fall off any second.

A second light came on. Now that there were two lights, Wyatt could see more people. He had to get this under control now, or his crime scene would be totally contaminated.

"Hey!" Wyatt grabbed the kid's arm.

"Ow, dude. Watch the shirt."

"Where's the deputy sheriff?"

"I don't know." The kid shrugged and peered up at Wyatt from under his cap. "What's the nine-one-one?"

"The nine-one-one is you're stomping on my crime scene. Who the hell authorized you to be here?"

"My boss the hell did, dude."

Wyatt tightened his fist in the boy's shirt. "I'm not *dude*. I'm Lieutenant Wyatt Colter, Texas Ranger. Now, who authorized you to be here?"

The kid's eyes bugged out. "I, uh, I'm an anthropology major. This is part of my Forensics 4383 course. If we're lucky, we'll see signs of murder on the bones."

Wyatt's anger skyrocketed. He twisted his fist in the kid's shirt, showing him he didn't appreciate his comment.

"Those are human beings," he growled. "Show some respect."

"Y-yes, sir."

Forensics course. He should have guessed. The students were from Texas State. They were here with Dr. George *Something,* the head of the Forensics Department. He'd been called in by Wyatt's captain. And without asking, he'd brought a bunch of ghoulish kids with him.

No way was Wyatt going to allow students to stomp all over this scene. He had a very good reason for

wanting to make sure nothing—and that meant *nothing*—
went wrong.

This time.

As the head of the Texas Rangers Special Investigations Unit, Wyatt hadn't been surprised when he was
assigned to investigate a suspicious shallow grave containing badly decomposed remains. What had surprised
him was that his assignment was in this town.

The last time Wyatt had seen Comanche Creek, it
had been through a haze of pain and the stench of
failure as he was loaded into an ambulance two years
ago.

The idea that he was here now, to possibly identify
the body of the woman he'd failed to protect back then,
ignited a burning in his chest. He absently rubbed the
scar under his right collarbone.

"Where's your boss?" he snapped.

"Over there."

Wyatt looked in the general direction of the kid's
nod. There was a group of people standing inside the
tape, right in the middle of his crime scene. He caught
flashes of light as one of them took pictures.

"Which one?"

"In the hoodie."

Wyatt raised his arm an inch, nearly lifting the kid off
his feet. All three had on hooded sweatshirts. "Try
again."

"Ow, dude! I mean, sir. The black hoodie. Taking
pictures."

Wyatt let go of the kid and turned on his heel.

So the forensic anthropologist was going to be his
first problem. He was the only member of the task force
that Wyatt knew nothing about. He'd been appointed by
the captain.

Wyatt had chosen the rest of the team. He'd picked Reed Hardin, the sheriff of Comanche Creek, and Jonah Becker's daughter Jessie, because of their familiarity with the area. He had hopes that Ranger Sergeant Cabe Navarro's presence would ease the tension between the Caucasian and Native American factions in town.

He'd never worked with Ranger Crime Scene Analyst Olivia Hutton, but she had an excellent reputation, even if she was from back East.

It was the captain's idea to use an anthropologist from Texas State University. "They have one of the premier forensics programs in the United States," he'd told Wyatt.

"And besides, the governor's looking for positive press for the new forensics building and body farm Texas State just built."

Great. Politics. That was what Wyatt had thought at the time. And now his fears were realized. The professor was trying to take over his crime scene.

"Well, Dr. Mayfield," Wyatt muttered. "You might be the head of your little world, but you're in my world now."

As he strode over to confront the professor, he took in the circus the guy had brought with him. Two spotlight holders, plus four other students milling around. Add to that three rubberneckers drooling over his crime scene, and it equaled nine people. And that was eight— nearly nine, too many.

He stopped when the scuffed toes of his favorite boots were less than five inches from the professor's gloved hand and toeing the edge of a shallow, lumpy mud hole.

"Hey, Professor."

The guy had hung his camera around his neck and was now holding a high-intensity pocket flashlight. He shone it on Wyatt's tooled leather boots for a second, then aimed it at a white ruler with large numbers on it, propped next to what looked to Wyatt like a ridge of dirt.

"Okay," Wyatt muttered to himself, pulling his own flashlight out and thumbing it on. *En garde*. He crossed the other man's beam with his own. "Hey. Excuse me, *Professor?*" he said loud enough that heads turned from the farthest spotlight pole.

Wyatt heard drops of rain spattering on the brim of his Stetson as the guy thumbed off the flashlight and pushed his hoodie back. Wyatt spotted a black ponytail. *Oh, hell.* This was no gray-haired scholar with a tweed jacket and Mister Magoo glasses. He was a long-haired hippie type.

Just what he needed, along with everything else. He hoped the guy didn't have a *cause* that could interfere with this investigation.

The professor rose from his haunches and lifted his head.

"Hey to you." The voice was low and throaty.

Low, throaty and undeniably feminine. Wyatt blinked. It matched the pale, oval, feminine face, framed by a midnight-black crown of hair pulled haphazardly back into a ponytail.

He'd heard that voice, seen that face, wished he could touch that hair, before.

"Oh, hell," he whispered.

"Yes, you already said that."

Had he? Out loud? He clamped his jaw.

She turned to look at the kid with the spotlight. "Let's get that canopy back up. It's starting to rain."

Then she gestured to the two standing beside her. "Help them. No. Leave my kit here."

Then she tugged off her gloves and wiped a slender palm from her forehead back to the crown of her head. The gesture smoothed away the strands of hair that had been stuck to her damp skin, along with several starry droplets of rain.

Wyatt wasn't happy that he remembered how hard she had to work to tame that hair.

"I have to say, though, I'm really fond of *hey*. You're just as eloquent and charming as I remember," she said.

He felt irritation ballooning in his chest. He could show her eloquent and charming.

No. Screw it. She didn't deserve to see his charming side. Ever.

"The name listed on the task force was George Mayfield, from some university. *Not* Nina Jacobson," he informed her.

Her lips, which were annoyingly red, turned up. "Texas State. And that's right. It was supposed to be George Mayfield. Think of this as a last-minute change."

"I'm thinking of it as a long, thick string being pulled. Where's Spears?"

"Who?"

"The deputy who's supposed to be guarding my crime scene."

"Oh. Of course. Kirby." She smiled. "He's very helpful. I told him he could leave."

"And he *did?*"

She nodded.

He was about two seconds away from exploding. He lowered his head, and water poured off the brim of his Stetson, onto her pants.

"Oh!" she cried, brushing at them. "You did that on purpose."

"I wish," he said firmly, working hard not to smile. "I want these people out of here."

"No."

"What? Did you just say no?"

"That's right. *No.* I need them here. It's already started to sprinkle rain. If we're not careful, we're going to lose evidence."

That reminded him of what she had said about the canopy. "You took down the canopy? Have you totally contaminated the scene?"

"The canopy was collapsing. It was about to dump gallons of water right into the middle of the site."

He glowered at her. "Well, I'm not having a bunch of college brats stomping all over my crime scene. This is not a field trip. It's serious business. More serious than you may know."

Nina's pretty face stiffened, as did her sweatshirt-clad shoulders and back. "I am perfectly aware of how serious this find is. You, of all people, should understand just *how* aware I am."

Now his eyes were burning as badly as his chest. He squeezed them shut for a second and took a deep breath, trying to rein in his temper. "Get them out of here," he said slowly and evenly.

Nina's eyes met his and widened. To her credit, she lifted her chin. But she also swallowed nervously, and her hand twitched. She showed great control in not lifting it to clutch at her throat.

But then, she'd always showed admirable control, unlike her best friend, Marcie. It had baffled him how the two of them—so completely different—had ever become so close.

He held her gaze, not an easy task with those intimidating dark eyes, until she faltered and looked away.

He'd gotten to her, and he was glad. Last time they'd seen each other, she'd had the final word.

It's your fault. My best friend could be dead, and it's all your fault. You were supposed to protect her.

She stepped past him with feminine dignity and walked over to the kid whose pants were still drooping.

He heard him say, "Yes, ma'am." Then he heard her say, "Okay, guys. Let's put this equipment away. We're done for the night. We'll get started again in the morning."

Wyatt turned and found Nina staring at him. "They're done, period, Professor."

This time her chin went up and stayed up. "We'll see about that tomorrow, Lieutenant. And I'm not a professor. I'm a fellow."

Wyatt felt a mean urge and acted on it before his better judgment could stop him. He shook his head. "No, Professor, you're definitely *not* a fellow. I can attest to that."

"Go to hell," she snapped.

"Charming," he muttered.

She turned away, so quickly that her ponytail almost slapped her in the face, and followed the students to the SUVs.

Wyatt took off his hat and slung the water off the brim, ran a hand through his hair, then seated the Stetson back on his head. The rain had settled into a miserable drizzle, the drops falling just fast enough to seep through clothes and just slow enough to piss him off.

He went back to the Jeep and got a roll of crime-scene tape. Obviously one thickness of yellow tape around the perimeter wasn't warning enough. Not that twenty thicknesses would actually keep anyone from getting to the newly discovered grave, but the tape, plus the deputy, who was supposed to be here by midnight and guard the scene until morning, would be a deterrent.

At least for law-abiding folks.

By the time he was finished retaping the perimeter, three times over, most of the equipment was gone from the site and the two SUVs had loaded up and left.

He looked at his watch. Eleven o'clock. An hour until Sheriff Hardin's second deputy arrived. He debated calling Hardin and reaming him and his deputy for leaving the crime scene unguarded. But he could just as easily do that tomorrow morning.

He crossed his arms and surveyed the scene. At least the rain had stopped for the moment. He took off his hat again and slapped it against his thigh, knocking more water off the brim, then seated it back on his head.

Propping a boot on top of a fallen tree trunk, he stared down at the shallow, jagged hole in the ground, his mood deteriorating.

The rain had released more odors into the air. The fresh smell of newly turned earth was still there, seasoned with the sharp scent of evergreen and the fresh odor of rain-washed air. Still, he couldn't shake the sensation that he could smell death. Even if he knew bones didn't smell.

A frisson of revulsion slid through him, followed immediately by remorse. He propped an elbow on his knee and glared at the hole, as if he could bully it into giving up its secrets.

Are you down there, Marcie?

So now he was talking to dead people? He reined in

his runaway imagination sharply. If the remains unearthed here were those of his missing witness, Marcie James, at least her family and friends would have closure.

And he would know for sure that his negligence had gotten her killed. As always, he marveled at his unrealistic hope that somehow Marcie had survived the attack that had nearly killed him. Still, he recognized it for what it was—a last-ditch effort by his brain to protect him from the truth.

She was dead and it was his fault.

He heard the voices arguing with his, like they always did. His captain, assuring him that the Rangers' internal investigation had exonerated him of any negligence. The surgeon who'd worked for seven hours to repair the damage to his lung from the attacker's bullet, declaring that he ought to be a dead man.

But louder than all of them was the one low, sexy voice that agreed with him. The voice of Nina Jacobson.

My best friend is gone. She could be dead, and it's all your fault. You were supposed to protect her.

He rubbed his chin and tried to banish her words from his brain. He needed to put the self-recrimination and regret behind him. Whether or not Marcie James's death was his fault wasn't the issue now.

Identifying whoever was buried in this shallow hole was. For a few moments, he got caught up in examining the scene. This was the first time he'd seen it. The kids had erected the canopy, so the area underneath was dark.

But Wyatt could imagine what had happened. The road crew that was breaking ground for the controversial new state route that cut across this corner of Jonah Becker's land had brought in its bulldozer. It had dug into this rise and unearthed the bones.

The discovery of the bodies—combined with the fact that the ME couldn't make a definitive identification of the age, sex or time of death of any of the victims—had reopened a lot of old wounds in Comanche Creek.

Marcie James's kidnapping and disappearance two years before had been the latest of several such incidents in the small community in recent years.

About three years prior to Marcie's disappearance, an antiques broker who had been accused of stealing Native American artifacts from Jonah Becker's land had disappeared, along with several important pieces. Everyone thought Mason Lattimer had skipped town with enough stolen treasure to set him up for life. But none of the pieces had ever surfaced.

Then, less than a year after Lattimer's disappearance, a Native American activist leader named Ray Phillips had vanished into thin air after a confrontation with Comanche Creek's city council and an argument with Jonah Becker.

One odd character vanishing was a curiosity. A second disappearance was noteworthy. But a third in five years?

That the third person was an innocent young woman scheduled to testify in a land-deal fraud case connected to a prominent local landowner cemented the connection between each of the bodies and that landowner—Jonah Becker.

It had taken less than twenty-four hours to rekindle the fires of suspicion, attacks and counterattacks in the small community of Comanche Creek. The warring factions that had settled into an uneasy truce—the Comanche community, the wealthy Caucasian element and activist groups on both sides—were suddenly back at each other's throats.

Wyatt straightened and took a deep breath as he surveyed his surroundings. The moisture in the air rendered it heavy and unsatisfying. He unwrapped a peppermint and popped it into his mouth. The sharp cooling sensation slid down his throat, and its tingle refreshed the air he sucked into his lungs.

Jonah Becker and his son Trace had both protested the state's acquisition of this corner of their property for a newly funded road, although the state of Texas had paid them. From what Wyatt could see of the area, the fact that they wanted to keep it despite the generous compensation was suspicious on its face.

To him, the land was barren and depressing. Anemic gray limestone outcroppings loomed overhead. The worn path that served as a road was covered with more limestone, crushed by cow and horse hooves into fine gravel, which sounded like glass crunching underfoot. Scrub mesquite and weeds were just beginning to put on new growth for spring.

Wyatt knew that in daylight he'd see the new blooms of native wildflowers, but a splash of blue and yellow here and there couldn't begin to compete with all that gray.

He pushed air out between his teeth, thinking longingly of his renovated loft near downtown Austin. The houseplants his sister had brought him for his balcony were much more to his liking than this scrub brush.

Just as he started to crouch down to take a look at the area Nina Jacobson had been photographing, he heard something. He froze, listening. Was it rain dripping off the trees? Or a night creature scurrying by?

Then the crunch of limestone from behind and to the left of him reached his ears.

In one swift motion he drew his Sig Sauer and whirled.

Chapter Two

"Whoa, cowboy," a low amused voice said.

Wyatt carefully relaxed his trigger finger.

Nina Jacobson. Son of a…

He blew out breath in a long hiss and holstered his gun. "I told you to get out of here."

"No. You told me to—and I quote—'get them out of here.'" She lifted her chin and stared at him defiantly. "I did that. For now."

He set his jaw. "Great. So we've established that you can follow directions. Good to know. Follow this one. *You* get out of here. Now."

She shrugged. "No can do. No transportation."

His gaze snapped to the empty road where the SUVs had been parked. Then back to her. First her face, then her left shoulder, which was weighed down by a heavy metal case, and on down to her right hand, where it rested on the telescoping handle of a small black weekend bag.

Oh, hell. He raised his gaze to meet hers.

Her eyes widened, and like before, he was grimly pleased that he could so easily intimidate her. He knew the effect of his glare. He'd seen it in the faces of suspects, subordinates and, occasionally, friends.

"Then you better start walking," he muttered, turning and propping his boot up on the fallen tree trunk again.

"Not a chance, cowboy. I'm staying with my site. I need to get some more pictures." Her hand moved from the bag's handle to the camera around her neck.

"It's not your site. It's my crime scene."

She didn't answer. Wyatt felt a cautious triumph. Maybe he'd won. Of course, he knew he was going to have to take her back to town, so she scored props for that. But there was no way she was going to turn his crime scene into a field trip for a bunch of students.

No way. He set his jaw and got ready to tell her to get into his Jeep.

"The ME said *he* thought there were two bodies." She spoke softly, but her tone got his attention.

Reluctantly, he slid his gaze her way. "*He* thought? Does that mean you don't?"

She stepped over the crime-scene tape and dropped to her haunches at the edge of the hole. He started to stop her, but she'd piqued his curiosity, so he followed her and crouched beside her, sitting back on his heels.

She slid her narrow, powerful flashlight beam over the clods of dirt and debris left by the road crew. After a couple of seconds he picked up on the pattern she was tracing.

Across, up, down and back. Then she moved the beam back to where she'd started and traced the pattern again.

"What? What are you showing me?" he asked.

"Look closer."

"If I look any closer, I'll fall in."

She laughed, a sexy chuckle that impacted him like a bullet straight to his groin. Surprised at his reaction, he shifted uncomfortably and swallowed hard to keep from groaning aloud.

"See this?" She shone the beam on her starting point and slid the light back and forth, over what looked like a ridge in the dirt. "That's a human thigh bone."

Adrenaline shot through him again. "That?" He pulled his own flashlight out of his pocket. "How can you tell?"

"I'm a forensic anthropologist. Bones are my business."

"What else can you tell about it? Is it male? Female? Child? Adult?"

She shook her head as she fished a brush out of her pocket. She telescoped the handle of the brush and leaned over to run the bristles across the surface of the bone. The dirt covering the bone was a mixture of dust and mud, so brushing at it didn't accomplish much.

"It's not a child. But making all those determinations is never quite as easy as the TV shows make it seem. Now look at this." She swept the beam of light across and up, then back across.

"Another thigh bone?"

"Go to the head of the class, cowboy." The beam moved again.

"And a third," he said, tamping down on his excitement—and his dread. One of those bones could be Marcie's. "Three thigh bones? Everybody has two, so was the ME right? There are two bodies in here?"

"Not so fast. These closest two may be similar in size, but the three femurs are all different," she said, with the same lilt in her voice that he was trying to keep out of his.

"Three? You're saying they're from three different people?" He looked at her, dread mixing with excitement under his breastbone. *Three sets of bones.* Three people gone missing in the past five years. Was it going to be that easy? "That's three different thigh bones, laid out like that?"

She met his gaze, her dark eyes snapping. "Yeah. Exactly. Look at that placement. They're crisscrossed in a star pattern. I suppose it could be chance that they ended up like that." He shook his head, but she wasn't looking at him. She had turned back to the bones and was brushing at them again. She gasped.

"What is it?"

"I think this largest bone has a piece of pelvis attached. That could definitely tell us if it's a male or female." She leaned a fraction of an inch farther forward and brushed at the far end of the bone. "Damn it," she muttered.

"What now?"

"The ground's too wet. I'm going to have to wait to unearth the bones."

"I guess you can't just pick them up."

She laughed shortly. "No. There might be something attached to them—clothes, another bone, a piece of jewelry. No. I have to be very careful to avoid destroying evidence."

"But you're absolutely sure the three bones are different."

She sat back on her haunches and tilted her head to meet his gaze. "Absolutely."

"Are you thinking…" He couldn't finish the sentence. He needed to know if one of those bones belonged to Marcie James.

Dear Lord, he hoped not.

Nina's face closed down immediately, and he saw a shudder ripple along her small frame. She needed to know, too. He understood that. But she had a very different reason.

She shook her head. "I can't say yet." Her voice had taken on a hard edge—the outward manifestation of an obvious inner struggle between her love for her friend and her professional detachment.

She hissed in frustration as she collapsed the brush handle, wiped the bristles against her jeans-clad thigh and then put the brush in her forensics kit.

"I need to build a platform so I can get to the bones without disturbing the site any more than it already has been." She informed him. "I can't rule out the possibility that this is a Native American burial site."

"Burial site? Are the bones that old?"

She shook her head. "I don't think so. I'll need to clean them and test them to be sure. But the layout of the land around here is consistent with the places the Comanche chose for their sacred burial grounds. I didn't see the site before excavation started, but the level of rise and the general shape suggest the possibility."

Wyatt grunted. He'd thought the same thing as soon as he'd gotten his first glimpse of the scene. The thought had gone out of his head once he'd seen the kids milling around.

"As soon as I can study the bones, I can give you the sex and race. However, to estimate the time of death requires more testing and equipment. Fresh bones will glow when exposed to ultraviolet light. The fluorescence fades from the outside in over time. Still, my opinion right now is that these bones are recent. As soon as I get them cleaned up, I can look at them under my portable UV lamp. Then I'll take samples for DNA analysis."

Wyatt's chest felt tight. There were only a few reasons that DNA would do her any good. "For a positive ID," he said quietly.

Nina nodded solemnly. "For a positive ID."

Both of them knew whose DNA they were thinking of.

He stared down at the three ridges. "So, Professor, I guess you need your students and their spotlights to help you get the platform built and extract the bones."

"That's right, cowboy." Her eyes glittered with triumph as she stood and pulled a cell phone out of her pocket.

He stood, too. "Tomorrow."

"Tonight. You just agreed that I need them." She flipped the phone open.

"Tomorrow." He folded his hand over hers, closing the phone. A funny sensation tingled through his fingers. For a second he thought the phone had vibrated.

She looked at their hands, then up at him. "Give me one good reason why not tonight. I told you I need some more pictures, and I do not want anybody disturbing the bones."

"Because I'll be overseeing every stick, every bone, every clod of dirt that's removed, and I need some sleep."

"Speaking of clods," she muttered, pulling her hand away from his. "It's dangerous to delay. This rain could turn into a deluge and bury the bones again. Any disturbance of the site increases the chances for contamination."

A pair of headlights appeared, coming around the curve beyond a thick stand of evergreens.

Wyatt checked his watch. "That's Deputy Tolbert. I didn't realize it was midnight already. That settles it. He's here to guard the site tonight. He'll make sure it's not disturbed. You and I are heading into town."

"I'll stay with the deputy."

"No, you won't."

"But the weather—"

"No more rain in the forecast."

"I need to—"

"I said no." He didn't raise his voice, but there went her eyes again, going as wide as saucers.

He gave a small shrug. "You'll get more done in the daylight."

He could practically see the steam rising from her ears, but she pressed her lips together and nodded once, briefly. He knew she'd been informed that as the senior Texas Ranger on the task force, he was in charge, even of the civilian members.

"Fine," she snapped. "Can I at least call my team and let them know what I've found and what I'm going to need in the morning?"

"Be my guest," he said, putting his hand to the small of her back, his gentle but firm pressure urging her away from the crime scene.

They stepped over the yellow tape as Deputy Tolbert's white pickup rolled to a stop and he jumped out.

"Deputy." Wyatt held out his hand.

Tolbert ignored Wyatt's hand and eyed Nina appreciatively.

Wyatt watched him with mild distaste. He'd sized up Shane Tolbert the first time he'd met him, over two years ago. The designer jeans and expensive boots, plus what Wyatt's sister called *product* in his hair, had pegged him as a player back then, and from what Wyatt could see, nothing had changed.

"Nina Jacobson. Gorgeous as ever. I didn't know you were going to be here." Tolbert touched the brim of his hat, then glanced sidelong at Wyatt. "Lieutenant Colter." His voice slid mockingly over Wyatt's rank.

Wyatt stopped his fists from clenching. Tolbert grated on his nerves, but Reed Hardin had hired him, and the sheriff seemed to be a good judge of character.

Tolbert and Marcie James had dated, although they'd broken up by the time Marcie was tapped to testify. It didn't stretch Wyatt's imagination to figure out that Tolbert was one of the people who blamed Wyatt for Marcie James's death.

"So, Nina," Tolbert continued, "what did you find? Doc Hallowell thought there might be two bodies in there."

Wyatt shifted so that he was a half step between Nina and Tolbert. "She'll be back in the morning with her team to start examining the evidence." He felt rather than heard Nina take a breath, so he spoke quickly. "We're heading to town. I'll be back here by nine in the morning, if not before. You know the drill. Don't let anyone close except Dr. Jacobson and her team. Call me if anything happens."

Tolbert's eyes narrowed. "I do know the drill, *Lieutenant*. Happy to oblige."

Wyatt directed Nina toward his Jeep. He'd talk to Sheriff Hardin first thing in the morning about the burr under Tolbert's saddle. If Shane Tolbert was going to be a problem, Wyatt needed to know.

"I DON'T LIKE leaving the burial site unguarded all night," Nina said.

Texas Ranger Lieutenant Wyatt Colter took a sharp right onto the main road into Comanche Creek. "The *crime scene* is guarded. Or did you miss your buddy Deputy Tolbert? He was the one in the black cowboy hat."

"I don't trust him."

Wyatt's head turned slightly, and she felt his piercing eyes studying her. It took a lot of willpower to meet his gaze. Finally he turned his attention back to the road. "Any particular reason?"

"Other than how mean he was to Marcie when they were dating?"

"They dated for how long? A year?"

"Something like that. Maybe eighteen months. Long enough for Marcie to figure out what kind of man he was."

"And what kind of man is that?"

"A loser. A coward. An abuser."

"He hurt her?" A dangerous edge cut through Wyatt's voice.

Nina bit her lip. She shouldn't have gone that far. She really didn't have any proof of abuse. Marcie had never admitted any specific mistreatment. "She just said he could be mean."

"Mean how?" He slowed the Jeep as they passed the high school and turned onto Main Street.

She should have known better. Wyatt Colter wasn't the kind of man to dismiss anything he heard or saw without sticking it under his personal microscope. Right now he was focusing that scope on Shane Tolbert, and she understood why.

Tolbert was guarding *his* crime scene. Wyatt considered it his duty to know everything there was to know about the deputy.

Nina wasn't sure how or why she had suddenly become an expert on Wyatt Colter. But she was definitely not comfortable with her newfound insight.

Time to change the subject. "I'm supposed to have a room at the Bluebonnet Inn."

In the watery glow from the streetlights, Nina saw Wyatt's jaw flex. She almost smiled. He was upset because she'd deflected his question.

"With your students?" he asked.

"No. They're staying on campus at West Texas Community College. The college made arrangements for us to have one of their chemistry labs as a temporary forensics lab, so we don't have to drive for an hour each way to the Ranger lab each time we need something. That's why I was so late getting out to the site. I was setting up the equipment."

"Is a community college lab going to be good enough? I can arrange for a driver—"

"It's really nice. Brand-new. All the chemicals a girl could ask for, as well as sterile hoods and some very nice testing equipment. Obviously there will be specific sophisticated tests that can be done only at a forensics lab, but for the most part, it's got all the comforts of home." She smiled.

For a few seconds, Wyatt didn't speak. "So you're the only one who rated a hotel room?"

"Perks of the job," she murmured as he pulled into a parking place in front of the Bluebonnet Inn, a two-story Victorian with double wraparound porches and sparkling clean windows. It was one of the original buildings in town. "Wow. Betty Alice has really fixed up this place."

He didn't comment, just turned off the engine and reached for the door.

"You don't have to—" *Oh.* For a second she'd thought he was getting out to walk her to the door. But that wasn't it. His jaw action earlier hadn't been because she'd changed the subject. "Don't tell me you're staying here, too? Well, isn't that…convenient." She sighed. She'd finagled herself onto this project, knowing she'd have to put up with Wyatt Colter. Relishing the opportunity.

He'd been so arrogant two years ago, pushing Marcie to testify against Jonah Becker and assuring her that she didn't have to worry. That as long as she was under the protection of the Texas Rangers, she'd be safe.

Marcie had trusted him. Everyone had. And no wonder. Not only did the very large, reassuring shadow of the Texas Rangers envelop the entire state of Texas and everyone in it, but Wyatt Colter himself exuded competence, assurance, *safety*.

It was the first thing Nina had noticed about him when she'd met him back then.

From his honed jaw and the cleft in his chin to his confident, deceptively casual stance, from his intense blue eyes to the long, smooth muscles that rippled with reined-in power beneath his clothes, he was the perfect personification of the Texas Rangers. And as long as he was guarding Marcie, nothing could possibly happen to her. He'd promised her.

Well, something had happened.

And it was Wyatt Colter's fault. Her best friend was gone—likely dead—because he'd never once doubted his ability to keep her safe.

When Nina had called in a favor to get on this task force, she hadn't thought any further than her determination to be a thorn in Lieutenant Colter's side and to find justice for Marcie. She hadn't bargained on spending this much time this close to him.

Still, at least this way she could keep an eye on him.

While Nina's thoughts whirled, Wyatt got out of the Jeep and headed for the front porch. As he climbed up the steps, it started raining again. He removed his hat and slapped it against his thigh, then glanced back at her before disappearing inside.

She could read his thoughts as easily as if they were printed in a cartoon bubble above his head.

Open your own door. No double standard for Wyatt Colter. If she wanted in on the task force in place of George Mayfield, then she should expect to be treated like him or any other member of the team.

Little did he know, that was fine with her. Gestures like opening doors, holding seats, paying for dinner all came with strings attached. And Nina didn't like strings.

She was here in an official capacity. She *expected* to be treated like any other member of the task force. While it was true that there was a chance that the site could turn out to be archeologically significant, Nina wanted nothing more than to find out what had happened to Marcie.

Well, that and to keep an eye on Colter. Not that she thought he was less than honest and aboveboard. She just didn't want to take any chances. This find could remove the haunting grief that had enveloped her for the past two years.

Marcie and she had been paired as roommates at Texas State, and despite their very different personalities, they'd become fast friends. Marcie had been there for Nina when Nina's father died and when her brother was killed in combat in Iraq. She'd been Nina's family. There was no way Nina was going to pass up this chance to find out what had happened to her friend.

The town was split. Half of the people thought Marcie had been killed. Her kidnapping had never resulted in a ransom notice. She and her mysterious kidnapper had just disappeared.

The other half figured she had got cold feet and arranged the kidnapping herself to get out of testifying against Jonah Becker, one of the most powerful men in the state of Texas. But if Marcie were alive, why hadn't she contacted anyone in all this time?

Of course, Nina wanted Marcie to be alive and well,

but there was one huge obstacle to that theory. If Marcie had arranged her own kidnapping, that meant she was responsible for shooting Texas Ranger Wyatt Colter.

And Marcie wouldn't have done that. Nina couldn't see her shooting anyone. Not even to save her own skin.

Through the glass front door of the Bluebonnet Inn, Nina saw Wyatt glance back toward her. With a wry smile, Nina opened the passenger door and climbed out, leaving her forensics kit on the floorboard at her feet. She hefted her weekend bag by its handles.

Wyatt was disappearing up the dark polished stairs by the time she got to the front desk.

"Hey there," the round-faced woman said on a yawn. She'd obviously been asleep until Wyatt had slammed the front door. "I'm Betty Alice Sadler. Welcome to the Bluebonnet Inn. Can I help you?"

"Nina Jacobson. I have a reservation. I apologize for getting here so late."

"That's all right," the woman said, tapping the keyboard with her index finger. "I'm always happy to have a guest. Let me just look here."

Nina sighed. "Oh, I forgot. The reservation is in the name of George Mayfield, Texas State University Anthropology Department."

"Ah. Of course." Betty Alice eyed her curiously. "This is about those bodies on Jonah Becker's place." In Betty Alice's Texas drawl, the word *bodies* sounded sinister. "Will Mr. Mayfield be joining you?"

"No." Nina didn't see any need to explain.

However, Betty Alice obviously thought she deserved an explanation. She waited for a few seconds, hoping to get one, but Nina just stood there calmly.

"Well," Betty Alice drawled finally and hit a few more keys. "I'll need your ID."

Nina handed over her driver's license and glanced at her watch. Betty Alice yawned again and sped up the check-in process. Apparently she was ready to get back to sleep.

She handed Nina a room key—a real key, to room 204 on the second floor. "If I'd known you would be here instead of—" Betty Alice glanced at the computer screen "—Mr. Mayfield, I could have given you the pink room. I keep it for my female guests."

Nina winced inwardly as she pictured how the *pink room* would be decorated. She didn't need a pink room. She just needed a room. She was exhausted, and eight o'clock was going to come very early.

"That's very nice of you, but I'm sure room two-oh-four will be fine. Do you have Wi-Fi?"

Betty Alice beamed at her. "We surely do. My niece hooked it up—or whatever you do with Wi-Fi. *And* it's complimentary."

Nina thanked her and headed up the stairs.

"Say, Nina Jacobson."

She turned around to find the woman pointing a finger at her. "I thought I recognized you. You were Marcie's friend. I remember you were staying here when she disappeared and that Texas Ranger got shot."

"Yes, that's true," Nina said, forcing a smile.

"Oh, my goodness." Betty Alice's hand flew to her mouth. "I remember him, too. Lieutenant Colter was the one who got shot."

Nina nodded, doing her best to suppress a yawn.

"Oh, honey, run along. Here I am, just talking away, and you're asleep on your feet." Betty Alice shooed her toward the stairs and turned around to head back to her own room behind the desk.

When Nina got to the second floor, Wyatt was holding a full ice bucket in one hand and pushing his key into the lock of room 202 with the other.

He turned his head and his offhand glance morphed into annoyance as his eyes lit on the key in her hand.

"That's right," she said, brandishing the key with a gaiety she didn't feel. "Howdy, neighbor."

He scowled. "Good night," he said and went into his room and closed the door.

"Good night, cowboy," she muttered.

After an ineffectual attempt to get mud off her black hoodie and jeans, and a defeated glance at her favorite work boots, which were beyond any help she could give them tonight, Nina took a hot shower.

By the time she had slipped on a bright red camisole and panties and was ready for bed, her mind was racing with her impressions of the burial site.

She settled into bed with both pillows behind her back and the pad and pen she always kept in her purse. She rested her pad on her bent knee and wrote the date, the location and her name. Beneath that she jotted a note to herself.

Ref: report of State Highway Dept regarding unearthing of remains. Attach copy.

Then she let her thoughts float freely. She'd type up an official report later on her laptop, but right now what mattered was getting her first impressions down before she lost them.

Incredible find. Texas Ranger Lieutenant Wyatt Colter has claimed it as his crime scene, but it's likely to be of archeological significance.

Appearance consistent with indigenous burial grounds.

Important to note that condition of the find suggests a possible hoax. Three unique thigh bones, laid out in a star pattern. Accidental? Or placed by someone? All three femurs appear to be of recent origin. The largest is certainly male. But I need to measure and examine all three to estimate gender.

Nina stopped and closed her eyes. Bones were her business, but that didn't mean she was immune to the idea of handling remains that could turn out to be those of her best friend.

A wave of nausea slithered through her, and her eyes pricked with tears. What if one of the bones was Marcie's?

Marcie. Sweet and kind, but impulsive, and maybe even a little bit self-destructive. Definitely not the best judge of character.

"Oh, Marcie, what did you get yourself into?"

Chapter Three

Nina shook off the renewed grief over losing her friend. She couldn't afford to get emotional. She needed to concentrate on the bones.

She reached for her camera and viewed the flash photos she'd taken.

She tried to view the three thigh bones in close-up, but the exposures were too dark. She'd have to send them to Pete, the graphics expert at the university, to have them corrected and enhanced.

She glanced at her laptop. She ought to send the photos tonight so Pete could get to work on them as soon as he got in tomorrow. The sooner she got the enhanced photos back, the sooner she could make more specific determinations of age, sex and time of death.

Still, in the morning she'd be able to look at the bones themselves. She glanced at her watch and yawned. Tonight it was more important to get her first impressions down on paper.

She continued writing.

Bones too covered with dirt and mud to tell much more. Already dark when we arrived at the site at 8:30 p.m.

History. (See fax from Ranger captain.) Two days ago road workers were breaking ground for a state route on land owned by Jonah Becker when they unearthed bones, which the foreman suspected were human.

The foreman stopped the ground breaking and called Sheriff Reed Hardin, who called the county medical examiner. The ME found the bodies "too decomposed and mixed up to identify" (i.e., skeletonized) and requested help from forensics experts.

Because of the state of decomposition and the fact that three people have disappeared from the area in the past five years, Sheriff Hardin called in the Texas Rangers, who were responsible—

Nina paused, then crossed out that last word.

—who were involved in one of the disappearances. The Rangers put together a Special Investigations Task Force.

Nina paused, clicking the cap of the ballpoint pen she held. If the site was a Native American burial ground…

Her pulse jumped slightly. She couldn't deny her excitement. New burial sites were rare. A junior professor getting a chance to be the principal on such a find was even rarer.

In fact, she wasn't sure why Professor Mayfield had acquiesced so easily when she'd asked him to let her take his place on this task force. Maybe he already knew the site wasn't old.

That thought gave her mixed feelings. She'd love to have a significant find with her name on it. On the other hand, she couldn't forget the real reason she'd requested to be on this task force. That could be Marcie lying out there. If it was, then she deserved a proper burial, as well as closure.

Nina clicked the pen angrily. Who was she kidding? If her best friend had been murdered, she deserved *vengeance*.

Nina twisted her thick black hair in her left fist and lifted it off her neck. Glancing down at the pad, she saw that she'd written *vengeance* and then underlined it three times.

She crossed through it and took a deep breath. *Okay, Dr. Jacobson. Get it together. You're a professional.*

Plan: Tomorrow students will construct a plywood platform from which we can extract the bones with as little disturbance of the site as possible. Until I can determine whether the site or any part of it is of archeological significance (a historic burial site), I am compelled to treat the entire site thusly.

First order of business: take samples of the three femurs for physical examination, dating and DNA extraction.

Nina chewed on the cap of the pen and read back over what she'd written, but she found it hard to concentrate. At least she'd gotten her first impressions down. She could add to it tomorrow.

She set the pad and pen on the bedside table, set her cell phone alarm for 7:00 a.m., and then turned off the lamp and sank down into the warm bed. But light from a streetlamp reflected off her camera lens. She turned her back to it.

It would take only five minutes to transfer the photos and send them.

"Tomorrow," she whispered to herself.

Tonight, the camera taunted her.

Sighing, she threw back the covers and turned on the lamp. She retrieved her laptop and booted it up, then grabbed the camera and transferred the photos into an e-mail and sent it off to Pete.

By the time she was done, her arms and legs were thoroughly chilled. She turned off the lamp and dove under the covers.

Despite how tired she felt, it took her a long time to fall asleep. To her surprise, it wasn't thoughts of the burial site or the identities of the remains buried there that kept her awake.

The image that seemed burned into the insides of her eyelids was of Wyatt Colter lying in a matching double bed not forty feet from hers, his broad bare shoulders and torso dark against the white sheets. Was he also having trouble sleeping?

Even if he was, she doubted it was because he was picturing her lying in bed this close to him. More likely, if he were fantasizing about her, it was a dream of watching her mud-covered backside recede as he ran her out of town.

She sniffed and squeezed her eyes shut. She had no idea why she couldn't stop thinking of Wyatt Colter. Probably she was just too tired to concentrate on anything rational, and too excited about the case to calm her mind for sleep.

She concentrated on her breathing, counting each breath until she dozed off. But as soon as sleep claimed her, an image of Wyatt rose in her vision—in boxers. In briefs.

In nothing.

"Stop it, Nina!" she growled as she turned over and pounded the pillow again.

Finally her breathing relaxed, and her brain began to banish the sensual but disturbing images.

A SHRILL RING pierced Nina's eardrums.

She moaned and squeezed her eyes shut. It wasn't her phone. That wasn't the theme from *Raiders of the Lost Ark.*

Which one of her neighbors had gotten a new, hideously loud tone? She pushed her nose a little deeper under the covers.

"Colter."

The low, commanding voice reverberated through her. Her eyes sprang open.

Colter. Bones. Marcie. Her thoughts raced. Had something happened at the site?

She sat up and kicked off the covers, squinting at the clock on the bedside table.

Four o'clock in the morning. She'd been asleep for over three hours. It didn't feel like it.

"Son of a... No. You stay there." Wyatt's voice, even through the connecting door, was deep, harsh, commanding.

She held her breath listening, her heart fluttering beneath her breastbone. She pressed her hand against her chest.

Fear? No. She wasn't afraid of Wyatt Colter. Maybe a little intimidated by his larger-than-life presence. But her reaction was definitely not fear. Now, if she were a criminal, she'd be afraid. Or a subordinate who'd screwed up.

"Have you called Hardin?"

Something *had* happened.

She shot up out of bed, grabbed her jeans and pulled them on, balancing on tiptoe as she zipped and fastened them. She didn't even bother combing her hair, merely twisted it into a ponytail as she thrust her feet into her muddy work boots.

"Call him. I'll be right there!" Wyatt's voice brooked no argument.

Just as she pulled the Velcro straps on her boots tight, Wyatt's door slammed. The picture hanging over her headboard and the glass lamp on the bedside table rattled.

She shoved her arms into her hoodie and threw open the door to her room. Wyatt's broad shoulders were just disappearing down the stairs.

"Hey, cowboy. Wait for me!" she called.

His head cocked, but he didn't slow down.

She started out, then realized she didn't have her camera. It took only a fraction of a second to decide. If she went back, he'd be gone.

She vaulted down the stairs two at a time, landing at the bottom with a huff and a scattering of dried mud.

"What the hell are you doing?" Wyatt growled. "Go back to bed."

Betty Alice poked her head out from the door behind the desk in time to hear Wyatt's words. Her eyes sparkled, and she snorted delicately.

Nina's face heated, and she sent Betty Alice a quelling glance. To someone who didn't know what was going on, she supposed Wyatt's words had sounded suggestive.

"Go on." Wyatt sounded like he was shooing a disobedient dog.

"Not a chance, cowboy. Where are we going? Did something happen at the site?"

"*We* aren't going anywhere."

"You can't keep me away from my bones," she declared pugnaciously.

"*Your* bones?"

Now Betty Alice's pupils were dark circles surrounded by white.

"It might be your crime scene, Lieutenant, but I'm the forensic anthropologist. They're my bones." Nina lifted her chin. "That was Deputy Tolbert, wasn't it? Something happened at the site."

Wyatt blew air out in a hiss between his teeth and tossed a peppermint into his mouth.

"Got another one of those? I didn't get a chance to brush my teeth."

He glowered at her, but she kept her expression carefully neutral. Finally he dug into his pants pocket and pulled out a cellophane-wrapped disk and tossed it toward her. She swiped it out of the air with no effort.

"Thanks," she said. "I'll pay you back." She was pretty sure she heard another growl as he spun on his boot heel and headed out the front door.

WYATT DIDN'T SAY a word on the drive out to the crime scene. He was in no mood to deal with Nina Jacobson. Against his better judgment—almost against his will—he cut his eyes sideways. They zeroed in on that red lacy thing that peeked out from under her half-zipped hoodie.

The red lacy thing and the creamy smooth flesh that it barely covered. He growled under his breath as his body reacted to what his eyes saw.

Snapping his gaze back to the dirt road, he clenched his jaw and lifted his chin. *Forget what Nina Jacobson is or isn't wearing,* he warned himself.

He had enough on his plate right now. If there was one thing he knew, it was how to separate his personal and professional life.

Yeah. Separate them so well that one of them no longer existed. His awareness turned to the slight weight of the star on his chest. That star, with its unique engraving and aged patina, represented who he was.

Wyatt Colter, Texas Ranger.

And as he knew very well, there was no place in a Ranger's life for personal complications.

"Would you at least tell me what Shane said?"

Nina's voice broke into his thoughts. It was breathy and low—sultry. Like a hot summer Texas storm. Like her.

He didn't bother to answer her.

Shane Tolbert had sounded groggy, embarrassed and angry all at the same time. But that was nothing compared to how he was going to sound—and feel— once Wyatt had ripped him a new one, right before he did the same for Sheriff Reed Hardin.

Wyatt's first act upon hearing about the discovery of the bodies less than forty-eight hours ago had been to demand two guards on the crime scene twenty-four hours a day. Sheriff Hardin had countered that one guard per eight-hour shift was plenty. "Nobody's bothered the scene," the sheriff had said. "There were a few folks who drove up there on the first day, right after the road crew discovered the bones. Most notably Daniel Taabe and a couple of his cronies, who wanted to know if what the road crew had unearthed was a historical burial site. But after that…nothing. My deputies can handle things just fine."

Wyatt had requested the extra men from his captain, but the captain had sided with the sheriff.

Now, as he'd known he would be, Wyatt had been proven right. If there had been two men guarding the site, this wouldn't have happened.

He roared up to within a few feet of the crime-scene tape and slammed on the brakes.

To his amusement, Nina uttered a little squeak when the anti-locking brake system stopped the Jeep in its tracks.

He jumped out, leaving the engine running. He stalked over to Sheriff Hardin's pickup, where Deputy Tolbert was sitting on the tailgate, with Doc Hallowell and the sheriff hovering over him.

"Need to go to the hospital?" Sheriff Hardin was asking as Wyatt walked up.

Doc Hallowell shook his head. He reached inside the black leather bag sitting beside Tolbert.

"Sheriff," Wyatt said.

"Lieutenant." Hardin didn't look at him. He pointed a pocket flashlight at Tolbert's head. "That's a nasty cut."

"I'm going to stitch it right here," Doc Hallowell said, searching in his bag, "as soon as I can dig out my suture kit."

A doctor making a house call or a crime-scene call. Wyatt shook his head. Small towns. They were a mystery to him.

"What happened?" Nina asked from behind him.

Wyatt wished he could pick this damn crime scene up and transport it to a secure location. He desperately needed some time alone here. Just him and the crime scene, and maybe Olivia Hutton, the top-notch crime scene analyst. He could use her expertise, but while she was available to him as part of the task force, she hadn't been called in yet, since this was classified as a cold case. He made a mental note to call her and ask her opinion.

Tolbert looked up at Nina sheepishly. "Got myself conked over the head. I heard something and went to investigate. I'm thinking there were at least two of them. One to distract me and the other to bash my skull in." He winced as Doc Hallowell poured alcohol on the gash on the back of his head. "Ow! I guess I'm lucky I've got a thick skull."

From the corner of his eye, Wyatt saw the thinly disguised look of disgust on Nina's face. She *really* didn't like Tolbert.

"Doc," Wyatt said. "can I look at that cut before you start working on it?" He pulled out his own high-powered flashlight and shone it on the deputy's skull.

The gash looked fresh, of course. And it was edged by an inflamed strip of scalp, which disappeared into Tolbert's hair. As far as he could tell, it had been made with a honed-edged instrument, like the edge of a plate or a board, or maybe even a hatchet, if it wasn't too finely sharpened.

The doctor had trimmed the hair around the gash, and now he was stitching it, quickly and neatly. Wyatt watched with casual interest as he tied the stitches. He counted seven.

"Any idea what they hit you with?" Wyatt asked.

Tolbert shook his head. "No clue. Something with an edge. Maybe the back side of an ax. You see how much it bled."

Wyatt gestured to Nina. "Professor, can you get a couple of photos of the wound?"

"Hey," Tolbert said, ducking his head. "It's humiliating enough without a record of it."

Nina snapped a couple of shots.

"I need it for a match with a possible weapon," Wyatt explained.

"Stay still, Shane," the doctor said. "I'm almost done."

"They just hit you once?" Wyatt asked.

"Ow, Doc!" Tolbert exclaimed, blinking as Nina's camera flashed. "Are you done yet?"

Hardin took a step backward. "Lieutenant Colter? Looks like Doc's getting Shane fixed up. Why don't we check out the crime scene?"

Wyatt looked at Tolbert, then at Hardin. He had a lot more questions for the deputy, but the sheriff obviously wanted him at the crime scene—or away from Tolbert.

"You mean nobody has checked out the damage yet?" Wyatt replied.

When Wyatt turned to head over to the burial site, he saw that Nina was there. As he watched, she crouched down to sit on her haunches—the exact position she'd been in earlier.

Only this time he knew who she was. How could he have thought she was a middle-aged, sedentary professor of anthropology? Granted, it had been raining and she'd been cloaked by that oversize black hooded sweatshirt. But looking at her now in the same position, he couldn't believe he'd mistaken the feminine curve of her back and behind for a male's.

She pushed the hood of her sweatshirt off her head and shone the beam of her high-powered flashlight along the ground.

By the time they walked up beside her, she had sat back on her heels, her face reflecting disgust and anger.

"One of my bones is missing," she said.

Chapter Four

"Which one?" Wyatt burst out. "Which bone is missing?"

Nina shook her head. "Whoever did this made a mess. Tromped all over the site. But I think it's the largest one. The one that had a piece of pelvis attached to it." She looked up at him, her dark eyes snapping.

Wyatt shone his flashlight over the ground. "Can you get casts of these prints?" he asked the sheriff.

Hardin crouched down and studied the ground. "It's pretty wet, and he was slipping in the mud. But yeah."

"You're sure?" Wyatt asked.

Hardin nodded. "Deputy Spears can handle it."

"Make sure he finds the sharpest print," said Wyatt.

Hardin frowned. "Look, Lieutenant, if you want to call in your own crime scene investigator—"

"No!" Nina exclaimed.

Wyatt's gaze snapped to her.

"Sheriff, if your deputy can cast the prints over there, I'd appreciate it." She pointed. "I *really* don't want anyone else trampling the site."

Wyatt shook his head. "Professor—"

Nina stood. "First of all, I'm a certified crime scene investigator, so *I* can do it if you insist. But I have no doubt that Sheriff Hardin and his men know what they're doing. Let them cast the prints over there while I extract the other two bones. I'll process this area for trace evidence while I'm at it."

It probably couldn't hurt for her to handle the crime scene. And the boot prints at the edge of the shallow hole were clearer, anyhow. He nodded at Hardin.

Beside him, Nina sighed in obvious relief.

The sheriff rose, dusting his hands against each other, then propping them on his hips.

"Can we get them done now?" Wyatt asked.

This was why he didn't like small towns. Everything moved at a snail's pace. This was a crime scene— a major crime scene. It might tell them of the disappearances that had haunted Comanche Creek for the past several years. It might hold evidence of what had happened to Marcie James.

And yet the people who could provide the answers— the doctor, the sheriff, the deputies—seemed to operate with a "we'll get around to it" mentality.

Hardin sent Wyatt a hard glance. "Can we get a thing or two straight, Lieutenant?"

"Happy to. As long as it cuts down on the delays." Wyatt nodded.

"This isn't Austin. We might be kind of slow here compared to your Texas Ranger pace, but we can do the job," Hardin replied. "I've already called Deputy Spears and told him to get back out here. Once he's here, he'll get the footprints cast. Do you think that'll be time enough for you?"

Wyatt clenched his jaw. "That's fine. Spears. He's the one who abandoned the crime scene, isn't he?"

"He didn't abandon it." Hardin countered. "Dr. Jacobson, a member of *your* task force, assured him that she would be responsible for the scene until Tolbert came on at midnight."

"Nobody on *my* task force but me has that authority, Sheriff. Is that clear?" Wyatt grumbled.

Reed Hardin's mouth flattened, but he nodded.

Wyatt felt a twinge of regret for his tone. "Thanks," he muttered. "When can I talk to Deputy Tolbert?"

"Any time, Lieutenant. I would like Doc to release him first."

Wyatt nodded. "What's the story with him, anyhow? I know he and Marcie James were dating at one time. Apparently she told Nina he could be abusive."

"I said *mean*," Nina interjected as she bent down again to study the indentation where the missing bone had lain.

Hardin nodded. "Right. Abusive might be too strong a word. Shane's got a temper, but he's a good deputy. He's competent. Might even call him a go-getter." Hardin's mouth quirked up in a smile. "I wouldn't be surprised if he has his sights on being sheriff one day."

"You trust him that much?" asked Wyatt.

"Whether or not he could become sheriff has nothing to do with how much I do or don't trust him. It's a matter of competence," replied Hardin. "In fact, that's one of the things I admire about him. He's gone to school on his own time to take classes on crime scene investigation. He's pretty knowledgeable."

"Yeah?" Wyatt's mental radar buzzed. So Tolbert was *pretty knowledgeable* about CSI. "Where'd he get his degree in hostility?"

Hardin shrugged. "That he comes by naturally. His dad, Ben Tolbert, has always been a drinker and a woman chaser. Knocked Shane around some until he got big enough to fight back."

"And once he got big enough?"

"I doubt you're asking that question without knowing the answer."

Wyatt nodded. "He has a suspension on his record. Excessive force."

"It was a domestic dispute. Single mother's boyfriend came home drunk and decided to whale on her eight-year-old for leaving his bike in the driveway. He broke the boy's arm. Shane broke the guy's nose."

Wyatt looked at Hardin with new respect. Suspending the deputy was the right thing to do, but it couldn't have been easy to put a black mark on his record for avenging a child. Especially given Tolbert's own childhood.

"Ever hear anything about trouble between him and Marcie James?"

Hardin shook his head. "You know how people can talk sometimes. I remember once she hurt her arm. Claimed she'd pulled a muscle playing tennis."

"Did you check it out?"

"Doc said it could have been twisted in a fall."

"Could have."

Hardin nodded. "I kept an eye on her, but I never saw anything else. Shane seemed to care about her. I don't remember why they broke up."

"What do you think about the missing bone? Who in Comanche Creek would attack your deputy and steal one of the bones?" Wyatt looked toward the burial site, toward Nina. As he watched, she stood and shed the hooded sweatshirt, leaving her in nothing but the little red thing. He swallowed.

"I don't have a clue," Hardin said. "I know there were people who were upset about Marcie testifying in the land fraud case, but it's hard to imagine that any of them could have killed her."

"The professor says the bones are recent."

Nina tugged the red camisole down over her low-slung jeans as far as it would stretch, which wasn't far, then picked up a fallen branch. After testing it with her weight, she stuck one end into the ground and braced herself as she reached across the shallow mud hole. She stretched precariously, straining toward something Wyatt couldn't see.

"What are you getting at?" Hardin asked.

"Could Shane have faked the attack so he could destroy evidence?"

Hardin sent him a questioning look.

"Maybe he knows whose bones are buried in there." Wyatt spoke without taking his eyes off Nina. The scrap of shimmery red material rode up her back, leaving a good eight inches or so of bare midriff between its hem and her jeans.

"You're suggesting Shane killed Marcie James? No way. He was torn up about Marcie's disappearance."

Wyatt swallowed, trying to concentrate on Hardin's words. "I want to question him as soon as possible," he said gruffly.

Nina reached a fraction of an inch farther, and Wyatt got a view of the underside of her breasts. He winced. In about three seconds, she was going to fall face-first into the muddy crime scene—not to mention expose her breasts—if somebody didn't rescue her.

At that very instant, she almost lost her grip on the branch.

"No problem," Hardin answered. "You can talk to him later this morning at my office. Say ten o'clock?"

"Make it nine. I'll be there," Wyatt tossed over his shoulder as he stalked quickly over to the shallow hole.

He bent and scooped Nina up with one arm, grunting

quietly. She was more solid than she looked. And her breasts were soft and firm against his forearm.

"Ack!" she squawked as he plopped her down a couple of feet away, on solid ground. "What? You!"

She got her feet under her and stood. When she swiped at a lock of hair that had fallen over her brow, she left a trail of mud. "I almost had it."

"What you *almost* had was a face full of mud. You could have ruined my crime scene. As an *anthropologist*, I'd think you'd know that falling into the middle of a find would contaminate it."

"I wasn't falling."

"The hell you weren't. What were you after?"

"I'll show you." She lifted her chin and walked imperiously over to the edge of the shallow hole.

Wyatt tried not to smile as he followed her. She had no idea that she looked like a tomboy, with mud streaking her face and wisps of hair flying everywhere.

"Damn it," she muttered and turned back toward him.

No. He corrected himself. With the curve of her breasts and the delicate bones and muscles of her shoulders and collarbone showing, not to mention the outline of her nipples under the red camisole, a tomboy was the last thing she looked like.

"What is it?"

"I don't see it now." She patted her pockets. "I need my flashlight. It's in my hoodie."

Wyatt clenched his teeth in frustration as he bent down and retrieved her hooded sweatshirt.

"Here. You need to put it on, anyhow." He couldn't stop his eyes from flickering downward, to the top of her breasts.

"What? Why?" She looked down, made a small distressed sound, thrust her arms into the massive sleeves and wrapped the sweatshirt around her.

With an effort, he turned his attention away from her to study the general area where she'd been reaching.

She pulled out her flashlight and turned it on.

"What were you trying to reach?" he asked again, hearing the frustration in his voice.

She aimed the beam. "Something bright."

"Bright?"

"Like metal. I think it might be a piece of jewelry."

"Or a gum wrapper."

She shrugged, still searching with her flashlight. "Oh. There!" She held the light beam steady.

"That clod of dirt?" Wyatt squinted at the unsightly clump of mud and something fuzzy and tangled. "It looks like it came out of a sewer pipe."

"Can you get it? I want it intact."

"Let me have that stick." He put his weight on the branch, bending it slightly to test it. Then he leaned on it.

"Use this." She handed him a small tool.

"What's this?"

"A trowel."

He sent a glare sideways toward her. "Keep the flashlight on the clump of dirt."

Bracing himself, he reached. Her prize was farther away than it looked. She'd have definitely ended up facedown in the mud.

By stretching his shoulder nearly out of joint and straining his biceps, he managed to slide the blade of the trowel underneath the clump. Holding his breath, he lifted it. Then he eased backward until he was balanced on his own two feet on dry ground.

"Hold on," Nina said.

Wyatt froze. "What?" he snapped, his arm muscles quivering with effort.

"Just stand still for a minute." She held her flashlight in her left hand and a pair of tweezers in her right. She probed the clump cautiously.

Finally, she found what she'd been looking for, judging by the hiss of breath he heard. She fished a small plastic bag out of her pocket, slid her find into it, sealed it and marked it. Then she retrieved a larger bag and held it out for Wyatt to drop the clump into.

"What was that you put in the small bag?"

"That was what I saw. I think it's a necklace. Let me seal and mark this, and we'll look at it." He heard the nervous excitement in her voice. She quickly sealed the bag containing the clump of dirt and wrote something on it. Then she held up the small bag. "Hold the flashlight for me?"

Her fingers trembled as she held the bag under the beam. She turned it this way and that, and used her fingernail to maneuver the object inside.

Wyatt watched, trying to make sense of what he saw. A narrow chain of some kind. Shiny, like fine gold.

"Oh, dear heavens," Nina breathed. "It is…" Her voice broke.

"Is what?"

Nina looked up at him. There was enough light for him to see a suspicious brightness in her eyes. "It's Marcie's necklace."

Her words slammed into his chest like a physical blow. *Marcie's necklace.* He hadn't realized that he'd held out hope that Marcie could still be alive. That somehow, against all odds, and despite his failure to keep her safe, she'd managed to survive.

"Marcie's? How can you be sure?" He held his

breath, dreading her answer. She'd been Marcie's best friend. If anyone could positively ID Marcie's possessions, she could.

But she didn't answer him. Her attention was on the contents of the bag, and her hand was trembling.

"Nina?"

"Look at it." Nina held the bag so the flashlight beam sparkled off a cluster of tiny diamonds embedded in the clump of dirt.

Wyatt squinted. "Wait. Is that *hair?*"

She nodded and took a shaky breath. "Human. Long. Blond. And see the diamonds? They form an M. I know this is Marcie's necklace because…" Her voice broke. "Because I gave it to her." She took a shaky breath and straightened.

Wyatt met her eyes and found them stone cold and filled with hostility.

"That means," she said harshly, "that one of those thigh bones is Marcie's."

Chapter Five

"Let me have the necklace and the hair. I'll give it to Sheriff Hardin and then get you back to town. You're obviously freezing." Wyatt's voice was gruff, disapproving.

"No," Nina said through chattering teeth. She clamped her jaw and consciously relaxed her hunched shoulders. "You're not getting rid of me that easily. I'm keeping the evidence. You called me in to do the collecting and analyzing, and I'm going to do it." She kept her arms folded, so he couldn't see her shivering.

Her hoodie was only slightly better than nothing. It was damp from where she'd dropped it on the ground, and she could feel a glob of cold, slimy mud sliding down between her shoulder blades. In spite of her determination, she shuddered.

Wyatt's jaw tensed. "Technically, my captain called in your *boss*, not you."

Nina lifted her chin and glared at him. His gaze narrowed, as if he was tired of dealing with her.

She studied his rugged features. He wasn't handsome. Not by Hollywood standards. His jaw just missed being too prominent. The cleft in his chin bordered on too deep. His wide, straight mouth barely kept his nose from looking too long. And his eyes were a clear, dark blue that she'd never seen in eyes before.

And those eyes were on her.

"I tell you what," he said. "The Ranger lab has DNA on file for Marcie. Divide that sample with me, and I'll have the lab test it against Marcie's."

Nina's fist tightened around the evidence bag. His suggestion was entirely reasonable, so why was her instinctive reaction not to let one single hair out of her sight? As soon as the question popped into her head, she knew the answer. It wasn't that she didn't trust the Rangers, or even Wyatt Colter. It was that she held in her hand the answer to the question that had haunted her for two years. Was Marcie dead or alive?

Wyatt raised a brow.

Nina nodded. "We'll need a witness to oversee the transfer of evidence." She glanced over at Tolbert's pickup. "The doctor."

Wyatt fetched Doc Hallowell, and within minutes the division and transfer of evidence were taken care of. Wyatt made a short phone call, then came back over to watch Nina lock her evidence bag in her forensics kit, along with the record of transfer.

"The courier will be here within an hour," he said.

"Thank you." She folded her arms, feeling the chill of the early morning seeping under her skin. "You know, Marcie was my friend. All I came here for was to find out what happened to her. I can't abandon her until I know."

Wyatt's eyes darkened, like storm clouds obscuring the sky. "Your involvement borders on conflict of interest."

She held his gaze. "If that's true, then you being head of the task force is definitely a conflict."

"Come on," he snapped. "Let's get you into the Jeep."

"No." She shook her head. "I never should have left the site. I'm staying here until my students can build the platform and erect a fence."

Wyatt's blue gaze narrowed. "Like hell you are," he growled. "You'll be frozen solid long before daybreak. The sheriff's got it covered."

"The sheriff may have the *crime scene* covered, but the burial site is my responsibility."

"Nope. It's my responsibility. You are a member of this task force—at least for now. I'm the head of it. Do you understand what that means?" He looked down at her from under the shadow cast by the brim of his Stetson.

She pressed her lips together and stared back at him, losing a little bit of credibility when she couldn't keep her chin from trembling with cold.

"It means I can have you replaced."

"On what grounds? I'm perfectly capable of handling this job."

"You're of no use to me if you can't follow orders."

"Orders?" She bristled.

A corner of his mouth twitched. "Orders. Now get in."

She stood her ground. "I'm the forensic anthropologist—"

He took a step forward. "Get in the vehicle."

She backed up. "I have a perfect right to stay here if I want to."

"Get. In."

Nina realized everybody had stopped talking and was staring in their direction. She didn't dare take her eyes off Wyatt, though. No telling what he'd do.

"What are you going to do?" she snapped. "Make me?"

"If I have to."

"How?"

He lifted a hand to the brim of his hat and pushed it back about an inch, enough to chase the shadows away from his eyes. "I could shoot you, I guess. But that would be messy."

She kept her chin up. "I've already lost one thigh bone. I don't want to lose another."

Suddenly he was in her face. "You risk losing a lot more than a thigh bone if you stay out here all night. Now, do I have to pick you up and put you in the vehicle myself? Or are you going to go on your own?"

She darted a quick, involuntary glance around. Everyone was watching them. She felt the sting of heat as a flush rose to her cheeks.

"I'm a Ph.D. You can't just *pick me up* and *put me* anywhere. Everyone's watching."

Wyatt inclined his head, and his eyes sparked dangerously. Obviously he didn't care.

Anger sent blood rushing to her ears and scalp. "Fine," she snapped. "If you trust the sheriff to keep your *crime scene* safe until daybreak, I suppose I do, too." She tossed her head. "No reason for everyone to stick around until then."

She felt Wyatt's eyes on her back as she trudged over to his Jeep and climbed into the passenger seat. He'd left the engine running, and the warmth hit her chilled skin like the first blast of a hot shower. She shivered uncontrollably for a few seconds.

The temperature gauge on the dashboard computer read forty-nine degrees. Not exactly freezing. But her sweatshirt was damp, not to mention the knees and seat of her jeans. And that slimy mud was beginning to dry on her back. The temperature didn't have to be freezing to cause hypothermia.

She looked out the window and saw that every eye was on her. And they were all smiling. Even Tolbert. Her face flushed with heat.

Then, as she watched, Wyatt aimed his intimidating glare at them, and one by one, they turned their attention back to what they were doing.

She felt an absurd gratitude toward him, and that made her mad. He didn't deserve her gratitude, for two reasons. First, it was his fault the men had been staring in the first place. He'd been out of line threatening her, even if he was in charge. Second, her oldest, dearest friend was missing and presumed dead because of him. She wasn't sure what he could have done to stop the armed kidnappers who'd grabbed Marcie, but he was a Texas Ranger. He'd sworn to protect her.

As for herself, she intended to have him at her side when she analyzed those thigh bones, but not because she trusted him to protect her. In fact, her reasoning was just the opposite.

She wanted him there because if one of the bones was Marcie's, she was going to need somebody to blame.

WYATT GLANCED back at the Jeep as he headed over to talk to Sheriff Hardin. There was a glare on the rain-spattered windshield, but he could make out Nina's black hair. He didn't have to see her face to know her accusing eyes were following him.

He supposed it was fitting that he was saddled with her reproachful presence as he worked to get to the bottom of Marcie's disappearance. After all, he'd lived for two years with her voice in his head.

It's your fault.

"What did your bone collector find?" Hardin asked, cutting into his thoughts.

"A clump of hair and a necklace that may have belonged to Marcie James."

"Where are they? Get them to me and—"

Wyatt shook his head. "Nope. Nina's tagged them. She's got the chain of custody."

"Are you sure she ought to be doing that? She was Marcie's best friend."

Wyatt's hackles rose, but he knew the sheriff had a valid point. It was the same point he'd just raised to Nina. "I trust her for that very reason. She's determined to find out what happened to her friend."

Hardin sent Wyatt a telling look. "Word is she's already decided who's responsible."

Wyatt shrugged as if that fact didn't concern him. "Maybe. Can't say I disagree with her. Besides, whether we like it or not, these are cold cases. And with the state of the remains, it's more up her alley than CSI's."

"What did you need the doc for?"

"We need to positively ID the hair as Marcie's. So the professor divided the evidence into two bags, with the doctor witnessing the transfer of some of the evidence from her to me. I've got a courier coming to take it to the Ranger Forensics Lab. We have Marcie's DNA on file. If the clump of hair is a match, we should know within twenty-four hours."

The end of his sentence was almost drowned out by the sound of a four-wheeler roaring up. Wyatt looked across the road and saw Trace Becker, Jonah Becker's son, climbing off the vehicle and heading their way. He remembered Trace mostly because of his hair-trigger temper and the two-by-four chip he carried on his shoulder.

There was a reason Wyatt had recommended Becker's daughter Jessie instead of Trace to work with them on the task force.

Trace stomped toward them, his chin stuck out pugnaciously. "What the hell's going on, Reed?"

Hardin held up a hand. "Now, Trace, calm down."

"Calm down?" Trace stormed. "This is the second time I've been disturbed tonight. Around ten I saw so much light out here that I thought we had a fire. Now there's another commotion on *my* land, and nobody bothered to contact me to let me know what was going on."

His land? Wyatt opened his mouth, but Hardin beat him to the punch. "Did you come down here earlier, Trace?"

Trace took a split-second too long to answer. "Earlier? What do you mean?"

"When was the last time you were here?" Wyatt broke in, narrowing his eyes as he studied Trace's cowboy boots. There was mud clinging to the sides.

Trace scowled at Wyatt for a couple of seconds, as if trying to place him, then turned back to Hardin. "I ran out here this afternoon to check on the burial site. Spoke with Deputy Spears for a bit, then headed back to the house to finish up some paperwork."

"And later, when you saw the lights?" Hardin asked.

"I stepped outside to see what was going on and realized they were spotlights, not a fire," Trace replied.

"Yeah? And then?" Wyatt broke in.

Trace cocked his head. "And then I went back inside."

"You weren't curious? Worried about what was going on up here?"

"I told you I had paperwork." Trace growled. "Are you calling me a liar?"

"I'm asking if anyone can vouch for you."

"Vouch for *me?* What the hell? You've got a lot of gall, standing here on *my* property, telling me I need someone to *vouch* for me." Trace turned to Harding. "Who the hell is this guy, anyhow?"

Wyatt took a step forward. "Lieutenant Wyatt Colter, Texas Ranger. I'm in charge of the task force looking into the remains that were found on *your father's* land."

Trace turned on him, only to be stopped by Hardin's hand on his arm.

"We're just trying to find out what happened," Hardin said. "Now, if your dad or Jessie can confirm that you didn't leave the house—?"

"They can't," Trace broke in. "Jessie's out of town, and Dad…" Instantaneously, his whole demeanor changed. "He's not doing so well. And all this isn't helping." He swung his arm in a sweeping gesture. "Reed, I asked what's going on."

Wyatt studied Trace. He was barely holding it together. His fists were clenched at his sides, and despite the chill in the air, he was sweating. Was he really worried about his father, and indignant about the intrusion on the Becker spread? Or was he afraid of what the Ranger task force would uncover?

Hardin sent Wyatt a telling look, then stepped over and patted Trace on the back.

"Somebody hit Shane over the head. He called us as soon as he woke up. When Doc finishes sewing his head up and we check out what his attacker was after, things will calm down out here. You know we've got to do our jobs." As he talked, he maneuvered Trace toward his four-wheeler. "Why don't you get back down to the house and make sure your dad's okay? We've still got a lot of work to do here, but don't worry. I'll keep you in the loop."

Wyatt bristled at Hardin's kid-glove handling of Jonah Becker's belligerent son. He was half-inclined to grab him and run him in for making threats against law enforcement. But while this was his jurisdiction, Comanche Creek wasn't his town and these weren't his neighbors. He was an outsider, so he needed to maintain a cordial relationship with Sheriff Reed Hardin.

He arched his neck and consciously relaxed his shoulders. The sheriff's words had calmed Trace down, so Wyatt kept his mouth shut. He'd talk to Hardin later about getting Deputy Spears to check Trace's and Tolbert's boots against the tracks around the site.

The ground was damp from the rain. Unlike the limestone road, the mud ought to show every footprint and the tracks of every vehicle that had come near.

As Trace's four-wheeler faded in the distance, the sound of a big engine filled his ears. He turned and saw a pickup roaring up.

"That's Kirby Spears," Hardin said from behind him.

"The deputy who let Nina talk him into leaving the crime scene unguarded."

"Tell you what," Reed said on a sigh. "You discuss who can authorize what with your bone doctor, and I'll do the same with my deputy."

"I haven't met him yet."

"Let's take care of that right now." Hardin led Wyatt over to the deputy's truck and introduced them. Then he turned to Wyatt. "You're coming to my office around nine tomorrow morning, right? Woody—Mayor Sadler— just called me about what's going on. He'll meet us there."

Wyatt got the sheriff's message. They'd accomplished all they could for the moment, and since it was already after four o'clock in the morning, everyone was going to be sleep deprived and grouchy, anyway.

"See you at nine," Wyatt said. Turning on his heel, he headed for his vehicle. He still had to deal with Nina until he could get her back to the Bluebonnet Inn.

He climbed into the driver's seat, put the Jeep into gear and headed back to town. The heated air was laced with the earthy smell of mud and rain, but underneath those expected odors was a totally unexpected one.

The subtle scent of roses. He gave in to the urge to take a deep breath, even while he lectured himself.

Nina Jacobson was a distraction, not an attraction. His body disagreed, as the sudden tightening in his groin emphasized.

He clenched his teeth and pressed his lips together, concentrating on the dark country road. He owed it to Marcie to find the person responsible for her death. He couldn't afford to let anything or anyone distract him.

No way.

"What?" Nina asked.

"What?" His response was automatic.

"You said something."

Had he? He pulled up in front of the Bluebonnet Inn. "Eight o'clock is going to be here before you know it," he muttered, opening the driver's-side door.

He glanced over at her. In the pale glow of his overhead light, with those big dark brown eyes and her ponytail coming loose, she looked like a bedraggled puppy.

He had to bite his cheek to keep from smiling. There was a reason people couldn't resist puppies. He deliberately tore his gaze away from hers.

Nina got out, wrapping her hoodie around her. She grabbed her forensics kit and stalked to the front door of the inn.

Wyatt was there before her. He opened the door and

held it, ignoring her suspicious glance. "You've got the evidence, right?" he asked.

"Do I look like this is the first time I've done this?" As soon as the words were out of her mouth, she regretted them, because Wyatt's blue eyes sparkled with mischief, and the corner of his mouth twitched. "Well, it's not," she said quickly. "I've assisted Professor Mayfield on several cases. Even if you're not impressed by my credentials, you should be impressed by his."

"I'm thinking that's why the captain requested *him* for the task force."

She was not going to let him bait her. Not going to get drawn into an argument. "If you're so concerned about my abilities—"

No. Don't go there. "Call Dr. Mayfield," she finished lamely as she pushed past him to climb the stairs.

At the top, she fished in her jeans for the room key. Finally, her fingers closed around it, and she unlocked her room door. She felt a tug on her drooping ponytail. Her head whipped around.

Wyatt held out his hand, streaked with mud. "Looks like you're going to need another shower," he commented. "Try not to make too much noise." He yawned and checked his watch. "I'm planning on getting three hours of sleep before I have to get up."

Nina made a face at him, but it was wasted energy. He'd already disappeared into his room and closed the door.

She let herself in and turned on the overhead light.

And gasped.

Someone had been in her room.

Chapter Six

Nina's fingers flew to her mouth as she stared at the bedside table. Her camera wasn't where she'd left it. She glanced around the room, trying to remember if she'd moved it.

Her gaze lit on her weekend bag. Had she stuck the camera inside with her laptop? The bag didn't look like it had been disturbed.

She shook her head. No. Her last thought before rushing out the door to catch up with Wyatt had been that she'd forgotten her camera. She remembered glancing back at it sitting on her bedside table.

Stay calm, she told herself. This was a small-town B and B. Betty Alice certainly knew that Nina and Wyatt were gone. Maybe she always got up by 5:00 a.m. Maybe she'd come in to bring fresh towels, and decided that the camera shouldn't be sitting out in plain view.

Or maybe she'd just been curious about the pictures. Even Betty Alice, with all her homespun giddiness, probably knew how to view stored pictures on a digital camera.

She stepped farther into the room and glanced apprehensively toward the bathroom. What if whoever had come into her room was still here? Not wanting to look like a wimp in front of Wyatt, she stepped over to the bathroom door and flung it open.

Empty.

She let out the breath she hadn't realized she'd been holding. Nothing looked out of place in the bathroom. The towel she'd used was draped over the shower curtain rod, and the floor was still puddled with water where she'd stood to dry off. So Betty Alice hadn't come in to replace the dirty towels.

Turning around, she spotted her camera sitting on the lower shelf of the bedside table.

Again, her thoughts turned to that split second when she'd paused to decide whether to grab her camera. She shook her head. She hadn't moved it.

Someone else had.

She started toward it, then stopped, taking a deep breath. Her camera could have been moved innocently, but did she dare make that assumption? What if whoever had stolen the thigh bone from the burial site had deleted her photos or taken her SD card to remove any proof that there were three unique thigh bones there in the first place?

Her logical brain immediately offered up reasons why that didn't make sense. Surely the medical examiner had taken photos. And that begged the question, had the ME's evidence been tampered with?

She glanced toward the door that connected her room with Wyatt's. For a couple of seconds she considered not telling him. But if her pictures were missing, it could impact the case, and she could hear him now if she left it until tomorrow. So she rapped on the door.

At first she didn't hear anything. Then the screech

of old pipes assaulted her ears, and below that sound, Wyatt's deep voice, although she couldn't make out what he said.

She rapped again, and the knob twisted right under her hand.

He stood there with his hand on the knob. No shirt on, and damp, tousled hair dripping water onto his forehead and shoulders.

He had a towel in his hand, and he wiped its edge across his face and then looked up at her from under wet lashes. When he met her gaze, he frowned. "What's wrong?"

"It's probably nothing…" she began.

"What?" he barked, looking past her and into her room.

"Somebody moved my camera."

His eyes met hers as if deciding whether she was credible, then he pushed past her. When he did, she felt damp heat wafting from him and smelled clean water, fresh soap and peppermint. The combined scents made her knees weak.

Since when did water, soap and peppermint smell like a hero? And why would she even think of that word in connection with Wyatt Colter, of all people?

He slung the towel back around his neck, the gesture sending graceful undulations along the muscles of his bare back and shoulders. "Where is it?" he said.

He still had on his khaki dress pants, but the belt was gone and the pants hung enticingly low, just covering the curve of his buttocks.

"Professor?"

"What?" She blinked. "The camera? Oh, it's on the bottom shelf of the bedside table." She went around him, trying her best not to touch him, and pointed.

"There. The problem is, that's not where I left it. When I left, it was sitting on top of the table."

"Are you sure?"

She bristled. "Yes," she said icily. "I wouldn't have bothered you if I'd had any doubt. Was anything moved in your room?"

He shook his head, sending droplets of water raining down on his tanned shoulders. One drop hit the back of her hand. She rubbed it into her skin.

"Have you touched it? Checked it to see if they did anything to it?"

She shook her head, staring at the damp hair at the nape of his neck. A drop of water rolled lazily down the back of his neck. Her mouth went dry.

He turned to look at her.

"No," she said quickly. "No. I left it where I found it."

He crossed the room to the table.

"Should you glove?"

He lifted the camera by its strap. "You go ahead. Check to see if your card's still in there. This is the camera you were using earlier, right?"

"Yes." She still held her forensics kit in her hand. She opened it and pulled out a pair of exam gloves and quickly donned them.

Wyatt lifted the camera up to the light. "I can't see the card slot."

Nina took the camera in her gloved hand. "It's on the bottom. The card goes inside here." She pointed, flipped open the tiny hinged door. "It's still there." She pressed the preview button. "My photos are still here."

"That's good. What about the rest of your things?"

"I don't think anything else has been touched. My laptop is in my bag."

"You checked?" And there was that note of censure in his voice again.

"No. But the bag hasn't been moved."

He looked at it. "How can you be sure?"

"Because I'm sure. Before I went to sleep, I put the laptop in my bag and zipped it closed. It's exactly where I left it, next to the bathroom door."

"And are those—" he nodded "—exactly where you left them?"

Those were a pair of white silk panties.

Nina bent her head over the camera until her suddenly hot cheeks cooled off a little. "That's right," she said. "Exactly. What do you want to do with the camera? Fingerprint it?"

Wyatt took his time shifting his gaze from her panties on the floor to the camera in her hand. He shrugged. "We could, but I'm betting either it's been wiped clean or whoever handled it has no prints on file."

"Still, someone was in here. They obviously looked at the photos. What if it was the same person who knocked out Shane?"

He shook his head. "How did they get in? Your windows are locked from the inside, and the door was locked, right?"

She looked at the windows. They were locked. She hadn't noticed him studying the room. He was good.

"And nothing's out of place in my room," he noted.

"Are you sure?" She asked. It was a silly question. If he'd observed all that about her room in the few seconds he'd been in here, it was a cinch that he'd already given his own the once-over.

He didn't even bother to nod.

"Whoever knocked out Shane probably knows Betty Alice," she said.

"Unless she's right in the middle of all this—the disappearances, the theft of the thigh bone—she'd never let someone roam through here in the middle of the night."

"You think Betty Alice looked at the photos?"

"It makes sense. She or some other busybody that works or lives here. Betty Alice is the mayor's sister. This is a very close-knit community—make that two very close-knit communities—on one side, the Caucasian element, and on the other, the Native Americans. There was a lot of hostility between them when I was here before…" He stopped, and she saw his jaw tense. "And it doesn't seem to have changed much," he added gruffly.

"Then we should probably get out of here before she or someone else steals evidence or—"

"Whoa." He held up a hand. "Not so fast."

"You don't think we need to move?"

"To where? The dorm at the community college, with your students?" He shook his head. "I'd rather not. For one thing, it would cause a stir. Everyone would want to know why we moved. My suggestion is to keep all the evidence locked up. Back up photographs, notes and any other important information or transfer to a secure location." He gave her a tiny smile. "I doubt we have to consider Betty Alice dangerous. But I'd rather be here, so I can keep an eye on her. Who knows? The fact that she's the mayor's sister may come in handy for us."

Nina nodded. Everything he said made sense, but the fact remained, someone had been in her room and had touched her things.

"Are you okay?" Wyatt asked.

Nina frowned. "Okay? Sure I'm okay. What do you mean?"

"Why don't we change rooms? The chain on my door isn't broken. You'll feel safer."

"The chain?" She turned to look at the door to the hall. She hadn't noticed that her chain was in two pieces.

"Later this morning I'll let Betty Alice know that it needs replacing."

"I don't need to move. I'm fine." She gave a short little laugh.

Wyatt picked up her weekend bag, carefully avoiding the panties, and set it on her bed. "Still, I'd feel better. Pack up and we'll switch. Then if anything happens, you can just yell." He went back into his room.

Nina quickly packed up her things and took them through the connecting door into Wyatt's room. He was waiting for her.

"Okay. Not much time left until daybreak," he said. "Make the most of it."

"I've still got to take a shower," she said on a sigh.

The look he gave her was fleeting but intense. "There's a clean towel in there."

Then he stepped through the door. "See ya later," he muttered.

Once the door was closed, Nina set her weekend bag on the floor and opened it, moving her laptop to get to her clothes.

She sighed as she stepped into the bathroom. If she didn't literally have mud drying on her back, she'd skip the shower and fall straight into bed.

Oh, no. The bathroom was still warm and steamy. The clean, fresh, minty scent of him permeated the air. A shiver that had nothing to do with the temperature skittered through her. Her knees went wobbly again.

For a few seconds, she stared at the damp towel he'd

folded and left on the back of the toilet. It took will-power not to pick it up and hold it to her nose. It would be warm and clean and minty, like him.

With stoic deliberation, she left the towel where it was. She turned on the shower and took out her rose-scented shampoo and body wash. Taking the cap off the shampoo, she breathed deeply of its sweet, familiar scent.

A slight breath of mint didn't have a chance against a bottle full of roses, she hoped as she peeled off her muddy sweatshirt and jeans.

WYATT STARED AT the rumpled bedclothes and thought about Nina in that little red camisole and red panties scooting around between those sheets, trying to get comfortable.

He was pretty sure just from looking at her that she wasn't the kind of woman who'd wear underwear that didn't match. Or maybe he just hoped she wasn't, because some day he'd like to see her in red bikini panties and nothing else—or maybe black ones. Of course, snowy white would work, too.

He swallowed and debated placing his head under the water faucet again—this time with cold water running.

He pushed his fingers through his damp hair, then rubbed the back of his neck and sighed. If he was planning to get any sleep tonight—today—he needed to get to it. A glance toward the connecting door told him it was closed. He'd noticed when he'd first entered the room that, although there was a keyhole in the door, there was no key. He'd checked to see if his room key fit it. It didn't.

As he'd climbed the stairs last evening, he'd overheard Nina declining Betty Alice's offer of what she'd called the pink room. With a grimace, Wyatt formed a mental picture of that room. He smiled at her quick refusal. Nope. He couldn't picture her in pink. Not with that midnight black hair and those sultry lips.

She just wasn't a pink kind of woman.

Purple maybe. Black definitely. And he'd like to see her creamy skin in that color that seemed to disappear... Didn't they call it nude?

But the red was his favorite. Bloodred. Like rich, velvety roses.

Any more of this kind of thinking and he was going to have to douse more than his head in cold water.

It took him only a couple of seconds to straighten out the bedclothes. Then he stalked over to the opposite side of the double bed and pulled the covers back and lay down.

But to his dismay, the other side of the bed wasn't far enough. His nostrils were still filled with the scent of roses, and when he turned over, he somehow ended up with a long black hair tickling his cheek.

He punched his pillow and turned over again. Even so, every time he managed to drift off to sleep, some part of Nina's body rose up in his mental vision.

Her breasts, their gentle swell hidden and yet highlighted by the shimmery red camisole she'd had on. Her bottom, barely covered by the low-slung jeans.

He knew nothing about her. He'd only met her three times. Once at dinner with Marcie and him, during which Marcie seemed to be trying to fix the two of them up. Then on that awful day when Marcie was kidnapped.

And last night.

He took a deep breath. Running around in a slinky,

revealing little camisole didn't fit his perception of her. However, being so excited about a forensic find that she forgot what she was wearing—*and* didn't notice what she was exposing—did.

Growling, he groped along the bedside table until he found the little pile of peppermints he'd set there with the rest of his pocket litter. Grabbing one, he peeled off the wrapper and popped the mint into his mouth, relishing the cool, sweet bite on his tongue, and the way the sharp mint taste and smell banished the last dregs of roses from his nostrils.

He turned over on his back, threw an arm over his eyes and directed his thoughts toward the next step in his investigation. He was scheduled to meet with the sheriff and his two deputies at nine o'clock. And with Mayor Sadler. He'd mentioned wanting to talk to Trace Becker, but they hadn't arranged anything.

Wyatt considered calling Hardin to make sure Trace would be there, but it was just after six in the morning, and he was pretty sure the sheriff was asleep—or at least trying to catch a nap.

Two hours. Wyatt took a deep breath. He had two hours to nap. He changed position again and tried to wipe his brain clean of thoughts and images. He even managed to stop thinking about Nina's body. The only image he wasn't successful in banishing was the look on her face when he'd opened the connecting door.

She'd looked terrified.

The trouble was, she'd seemed only slightly less frightened when he'd closed it after they'd switched rooms.

He couldn't blame her for not feeling safe with him. After all, they were here now because he had failed to keep Marcie James safe two years ago.

This time, no matter what he had to do, no matter what the cost, he would not fail.

He'd find Marcie—or her killer. And while he was at it, he'd make sure nothing happened to Nina.

Chapter Seven

Just before nine o'clock, Wyatt walked up to the two-story white limestone building with a triple arched front. Looking at it, he had the same reaction he'd had two years ago. It was hard to believe it was really the sheriff's office.

To Wyatt, it looked more like a facade for an old-style Western movie. He paused with his hand on the glass doorknob and checked the sign again.

"It's the right place," an enticingly deep feminine voice said behind him.

Wyatt turned and met a pair of dark, snapping eyes in a heart-shaped face framed by straight black hair. Her lips were bright red and matched the red shirt she had on. The rest of her outfit, a leather fringed vest, suede gauchos and tooled leather boots, might have looked costumey on another woman, but she carried it off like a star.

"I know, but it still feels like I'm walking into the middle of an old Western movie."

"I'm Ellie Penateka," she said, holding out a perfectly manicured hand.

Wyatt didn't know the name, but he was pretty sure he'd seen her before, back when he was here guarding Marcie James. She'd be hard to miss anywhere. He grasped her hand briefly, then pushed the door open and stepped back to let her enter first. "Nice to meet you," he muttered.

"We'll see," she whispered. She sent him a wink as she walked past.

Wyatt followed her down a wide hallway and through a door located midway. A young woman with dark red hair looked up and smiled at Ellie, then stood and gave him the once-over.

"You must be Lieutenant Colter," she said. "Sheriff Hardin is waiting for you. Through there."

Wyatt let Ellie lead as they walked through a small office with two desks—probably the deputies' office.

When Ellie opened the door marked Sheriff, Wyatt stopped in dismay. The room was crammed full of people. He frowned as he zeroed in on Sheriff Hardin, sitting behind his desk.

Hardin shrugged. He looked as irritated as Wyatt felt.

Wyatt paused for a couple of seconds to take an inventory.

On the opposite end of the room from Hardin's desk, Shane Tolbert sported a bandage on the side of his head and was soaking up sympathy from a man and a woman Wyatt didn't recognize.

He did know the large man with the weathered, rugged face and salt-and-pepper hair, whose hip was propped on the edge of Hardin's desk. It was Woody Sadler, the mayor of Comanche Creek and, from what he recalled, a very good friend of Hardin.

Standing next to Sadler was Jerry Collier, head of the county land office and Marcie's former boss. He was a weasely guy with a pinched face and a "don't ask me" attitude.

To Wyatt's left stood a medium-height, well-built man with ruddy skin and black hair anchored in a single braid down his back. He was dressed in a starched and ironed denim shirt and faded jeans. On his wrist, just above his watch, was a beaded rawhide bracelet. It wasn't a huge leap to the conclusion that he was Daniel Taabe, the leader of the Native American faction in Comanche Creek. He met Wyatt's gaze, and his brows drew down in a scowl.

He wasn't the only one. Everyone had stopped talking and had turned to glare at him. There were eight people in the room, and each one of them was packing their share of hostility. It hit Wyatt in palpable waves, like a hot, dry summer wind.

Hardin stood and stepped around his desk to shake hands with him.

"I thought we were meeting with Tolbert and Mayor Sadler," Wyatt said evenly.

"Apparently word got around. A lot of people want to know what's going on out there," Hardin replied.

Ellie crossed the room to stand next to Taabe. She said something to him, and he nodded.

"You know everybody?" Hardin asked Wyatt.

Wyatt nodded. "Most of them. Who are the two standing over there with Tolbert?"

Tolbert grinned and elbowed the man next to him in the ribs.

"That's Billy Whitley. He's the county clerk. And next to him is his wife, Charla," Hardin said.

Wyatt nodded. "Right. I remember the names from the transcripts. The DA questioned them about Becker's shady land deal."

"Marcie claimed that Billy was paid to alter some documents. But any proof that Marcie had…"

Hardin's words slammed into Wyatt's chest like the bullet he'd taken two years ago. Any proof of bribery connected with the land deal that Jonah Becker had tried to broker had died with Marcie.

"Where's Trace Becker?" Wyatt asked.

"I didn't tell him about the meeting," Hardin confessed.

"What about the boot prints? Did your deputy cast them?"

Hardin nodded. "Yep. Kirby will bring them in when Shane relieves him. He did tell me he thinks the boots are a size twelve. Same size Kirby wears himself."

"Any distinguishing marks?"

"Don't know yet."

"What size does Tolbert wear?"

"Twelve." Hardin looked at his watch and stood. "Folks, this is Lieutenant Wyatt Colter of the Texas Rangers. He's heading the task force that's investigating the bones found on Jonah Becker's land."

Wyatt felt the slight weight of the silver badge pinned to his chest as he met each person's gaze in turn. He took his time, staring into each pair of eyes a split second longer than politeness dictated. It was designed to make people uncomfortable—especially people with something to hide.

And usually, that was everybody. What they were hiding might or might not affect the case he was working on, but it was almost a cliché. *Everybody* had something to hide.

The only one of the eight who wasn't flustered was Daniel Taabe. He gazed back at Wyatt calmly.

Wyatt sent him a barely perceptible nod and turned back to Hardin.

Hardin opened his mouth, but before he could speak, everyone started shouting questions and complaints.

"Hold it!" Hardin yelled. "Just hang on a minute. Except for Shane and the mayor, every single one of you showed up without an invitation."

"Reed." Mayor Sadler stood. He didn't raise his voice, but everybody else in the room grew quiet. The mayor held out a big, work-roughened hand to Wyatt. "Lieutenant, welcome back to Comanche Creek."

Wyatt didn't miss the touch of irony in Mayor Sadler's tone. He doubted that anyone could have missed it. It was a cinch that, even if he didn't know them, they all knew him and what his connection was to the town.

He took they mayor's hand and shook it. "Thank you, Mayor Sadler—"

"Lieutenant," Mayor Sadler interrupted him. "Gathered here this morning are some of Comanche Creek's most prominent citizens. We're all concerned about the, uh…remains that were unearthed over on Jonah's land. What can you tell us about what's going on up there?"

Wyatt felt all their eyes on him. This wasn't his preferred way of working, but he'd make do. He'd never seen the advantage in meeting with a roomful of people, all asking questions at once. He much preferred to work one-on-one. He found it easier to draw out someone when it was just the two of them. He was intimidating, and he knew it.

Although he was a good judge of character and a good reader of body language, he knew very little about the people gathered here.

Wyatt took a deep breath. "I'm sure you realize, Mayor, that it's going to take more than a cursory examination of the crime scene and the remains to give us the information we need. We have a forensic anthropologist going over the entire area. As soon as she has definitive information that can be shared with the public, we'll let you know. In the meantime—"

"I've got a question," Jerry Collier said. "Just how many bodies are in that hole?"

Wyatt took his time answering. He met every pair of eyes in the room again, this time observing each person's reaction to Collier's question.

As before, Daniel Taabe's dark eyes held his gaze calmly. Ellie Penateka's dark eyes snapped with amusement and, unless Wyatt was badly mistaken, a touch of flirtation.

Charla's head was lowered like a bull's. Her lips were flattened disapprovingly, and her dark eyes gleamed with open hostility. Her husband, Billy Whitley, seemed to have a perpetual smile on his face—a distinctly unpleasant smile. To Wyatt, he looked like a hyena that had just finished a meal.

Tolbert gingerly touched the bandage on his head and averted his gaze. Wyatt was convinced that the deputy hadn't told him or anyone else everything that had happened out at the crime scene the night before.

Wyatt slid his gaze past Hardin to Woody Sadler. The mayor's deeply lined face looked worried and impatient. Next to him, Jerry Collier's beady eyes shone with excitement, as if he were about to learn a dark secret.

Well, Wyatt wasn't spilling any secrets today. He was here to gather information, not to impart it. So he wasn't about to get into how many bodies had been discovered or any other specifics.

"Mr. Collier, we don't know how many bodies yet," he finally said. "That's a question Dr. Jacobson will have to answer. And she won't be answering it until we've made a thorough investigation of the entire area."

"How long will that take?" Charla asked.

Wyatt shrugged. "No telling. I can tell you this, though. The fewer interruptions we have, the faster we can get to the bottom of this."

"What's that supposed to mean?" Charla snapped.

"It means just what it sounds like," Wyatt returned. "Last night, as I'm sure you all know by now, Deputy Tolbert was attacked, and the crime scene was compromised."

"We talk plain out here, Lieutenant," Billy Whitley said. "What the hell do you mean, *compromised?*"

"I mean, somebody stole one of the bones." Wyatt couldn't watch everybody at once, but he concentrated on soaking up the reaction to his words. His statement was no surprise to anyone in the room. Word had spread fast. "This is going to make Dr. Jacobson's job harder. Not to mention that whoever took that bone contaminated the crime scene. I have a feeling that was the attacker's intent."

Tolbert spoke up. "I gotta say, I feel really bad about letting down my guard."

A few murmurs of protest arose.

Tolbert waved his hands. "No, no. I should have been more alert. When I heard the road crew had dug up those bones, I figured it was another Indian mound. There's been a few uncovered around here." Tolbert turned his gaze to Wyatt. "It's hard to wrap your brain around the idea that some dried-up bones you're looking at could belong to somebody you knew." He paused. "Somebody you dated."

Charla laid her hand on Tolbert's arm in a comforting gesture.

"Now I have a question," Wyatt said. Since he was here, he might as well find out what he could. "Why would anyone pick that isolated corner of Jonah Becker's land to bury a body?"

The tension in the room went up several notches. Wyatt waited. Eventually someone would be compelled to break the silence.

It turned out to be Jerry Collier.

"That's a good question," he said eagerly. Wyatt noted the glare Charla aimed at Collier, who wasn't paying any attention to her. "That limestone road's old, from back when Jonah's grandpappy and everybody else got around on horseback. It's four miles from town, and it's far enough away from everything so that it's dark and quiet. For years kids used to go out there to park. Time was, everybody knew about Dead Man's Road."

Collier's words hung in the air. For a few seconds it seemed like nobody even breathed.

Dead Man's Road.

Then Mayor Sadler cleared his throat. "Jerry, it musta been you out there parking, although I can't for the life of me figure out who'd have gone out there with you."

Everyone laughed.

The mayor went on. "Kids today don't even bother trying to find a deserted place to park. Hell, they do everything right out in the open."

"Why do they call it Dead Man's Road?" Wyatt asked.

Collier answered. "Long time ago, an old Injun stayed in that cabin up the hill. Old man Becker let him alone. He died twenty years ago. My grandma says he must have been over a hundred years old. Most of the kids quit going over there when he died. I think they thought the cabin was haunted."

"Okay, folks," the sheriff said. "Jerry, if you're through spreading gossip, maybe we can get this over with. I hope you all feel better about what we're doing to figure out what happened out there. Now, Lieutenant Colter and I have things we need to discuss—official business relating to the crime. If you'll excuse us—"

"Sheriff," Wyatt broke in. "Since everybody's already here, maybe I could conduct a few interviews." He paused, observing each person's reaction to his words.

"What the hell?"

"Hey, I don't have time—"

"Is he accusing—"

"Hold it!" Mayor Sadler's voice quieted the small crowd immediately. He pushed the brim of his white Stetson up off his forehead. When he did, the rattlesnake tail attached to the band rattled. "Now, folks, we've got a heck of a problem here. You know it and I know it. Marcie James's disappearance was a tragedy. It's the lieutenant's job to figure out what happened out there on Jonah's land. Now, I'm going to guarantee to him that each and every person in this town will cooperate." He looked at each person. "I'm counting on you all to not make me out a liar."

There were low grumblings, but nobody protested.

"Who has time to talk to the lieutenant right now?" asked the mayor.

The room suddenly went quiet as a tomb.

Chapter Eight

The mayor straightened and cocked his head. "Now listen here. I said, I'm counting on you all. Shane, I know you can take time to answer the lieutenant's questions right now. And Jerry. Who else? Billy? Charla?"

Billy Whitley spoke up. "No can do, Woody. I told you Charla and I are headed into Austin today."

"No problem," Mayor Sadler said. "Just make sure you get with the lieutenant." He turned to Wyatt. "Well, Lieutenant. As you see, a lot of folks have places to go and things to do. S'pose you could schedule your interviews for later?"

Wyatt opened his mouth to answer, but the mayor wasn't finished.

"Tell you what. You can use my conference room next door, in the courthouse. The building's a dead ringer for this one. I'll even have my assistant set up the times for you. Just let her know when you're available and who you want to talk to." He slid a card out of his breast pocket and handed it to Wyatt. "Here's my office number. My assistant's name is Helen."

Wyatt nodded, feeling a little like a chastised schoolboy. Mayor Sadler had made all the arrangements for his questioning of the townspeople, and at the same time he'd manipulated him into doing it when and where *he*, not Wyatt, wanted it done.

Mayor Sadler was a sly one. Wyatt wasn't keen on questioning people under the watchful eyes and ears of the mayor and his staff, but in light of Mayor Sadler's perfectly reasonable compromise, any insistence on his part would only evoke more hostility.

Wyatt cleared his throat. "Sure. I'll just need to—"

The mayor settled his hat back down on his head and headed for the door. The small crowd took that as a signal and began to disperse. Charla and Billy took off, and Jerry Collier sidled over to Tolbert and whispered something to him.

"Lieutenant."

Wyatt turned. It was Daniel Taabe. Wyatt held out his hand. Taabe's handshake was firm, and he looked Wyatt straight in the eye.

"I understand Dr. Jacobson is treating the site as a possible sacred burial ground."

"That's right. I can't answer any questions about that, though. That's her area."

Taabe nodded. "Of course. I want assurance from you that any evidence you find will be discussed with me. As I'm sure you can appreciate, my interest is in protecting sacred Comanche rites and rituals, and preserving historically significant finds."

"The only thing I can assure you is that I plan to find out the truth about what happened out there. If I can, I'll see that you get the information as soon as I can release it."

"I'd like to be involved on the front end."

Wyatt nodded. "So would everybody else here. I can't give you special privileges, Mr. Taabe."

Taabe's black eyes narrowed slightly. "What if I

provide three men to help guard the site? One for each shift."

Wyatt eyed him. Just how trustworthy was he? Same question went for the men he was offering. The extra help would ease Wyatt's mind a lot. And if there was a Native American guard on each shift, along with local law enforcement, then maybe the result would be like the fox, the goose and the grain, and there would be no more midnight attacks.

He gave Taabe a slight nod. "I'll check with the sheriff. See what he says."

Taabe's head dipped slightly. "Good enough."

Beside him, Ellie frowned. "Daniel, he practically—"

Taabe moved one hand, an almost imperceptible gesture. Quieted, Ellie pressed her lips together tightly, but she didn't say anything else.

Taabe continued. "Lieutenant, one more thing. If it's all right with you, I'd like to talk with you somewhere other than in Mayor Sadler's office." Taabe's mouth turned up in a wry smile.

Wyatt nodded. "Fine with me. Where would you like to meet?"

"I'm headed to my office now. Would you be interested in talking there once you're finished here?"

Wyatt agreed and made a note of the directions to Taabe's office. They exchanged phone numbers; then Taabe and Ellie left.

As Wyatt stepped over to Hardin's desk, he noticed Collier had walked over to stand with Shane Tolbert. They were sharing a laugh.

"Well?" Hardin asked, dropping into his desk chair.

Wyatt shook his head. "Curious bunch of people," he commented quietly as he took in the area around Hardin's desk.

The Reader Service — Here's how it works:

Accepting your 2 free books and 2 free gifts (gifts valued at approximately $10.00) places you under no obligation to buy anything. You may keep the b̲ and gifts and return the shipping statement marked "cancel". If you do not cancel, about a month later we'll send you 6 additional books and bill yo̲ $4.24 each for the regular-print edition or $4.74 each for the larger-print edition in the U.S. or $4.99 each for the regular-print edition or $5.49 each f̲ larger-print edition in Canada. That is a savings of 15% off the cover price. It's quite a bargain! Shipping and handling is just 50¢ per book in the U.S̲ 75¢ per book in Canada.*. You may cancel at any time, but if you choose to continue, every month we'll send you 6 more books, which you may purchase at the discount price or return to us and cancel your subscription.

If offer card is missing write to: The Reader Service, P.O. Box 1867, Buffalo NY 14240-1867 or visit www.ReaderService.com

BUSINESS REPLY MAIL

FIRST-CLASS MAIL PERMIT NO. 717 BUFFALO, NY

POSTAGE WILL BE PAID BY ADDRESSEE

THE READER SERVICE
PO BOX 1867
BUFFALO NY 14240-9952

NO POSTAGE
NECESSARY
IF MAILED
IN THE
UNITED STATES

from the house. I ducked behind the car just as a bullet hit the car door. Then three more shots. I could see a shadow standing at the front door, so I pulled my gun and ran toward him but…" He stopped. His chest was tight. He took a long, unsatisfying breath and stood, looking out through the blue shutters on the windows.

"That's when you were shot."

"I hit the ground, but when I tried to roll up and shoot again…" He shrugged. He hadn't been able to get back onto his feet. There had been a two-ton weight pressing on his chest. He'd raised his gun and fired, but it was like he'd lost control of his gun hand. All he'd been able to hear were his wild shots hitting the wooden siding.

Nina spoke from behind him. "I heard the shots all the way over at the inn. Then Betty Alice's phone started ringing off the hook." He heard the clunk of her cup as she set it on the desk. "I remember that by the time I got downstairs, everyone knew you'd been shot and the sheriff had rushed to Marcie's house, but she was gone, and there was blood on the kitchen floor."

Wyatt turned. Her eyes were bright with tears. Somehow that hurt his chest more than the memory of the bullet's impact.

"I'd give anything if I could have been there to process that scene myself," he confessed. "By the time I could do anything, the house had been cleaned up and sold. I wanted to examine that door. The person I saw had come from inside the house. I'm sure of it."

Nina made a small sound. "Inside? Surely you don't think it was Marcie?"

He shook his head. "She screamed. I heard her say 'Don't shoot.' No. It wasn't her. But whoever it was managed to get into the house somehow—with or without her permission. And of course, the blood was

O-negative. Just like Marcie's." He rubbed his forehead again. "I've been over the files a dozen times. But that's not the same as being there."

Nina looked down at her hands, then up at him again. "Wyatt, I—"

"If there's anything you know—anything at all—tell me. About Tolbert, about Marcie. About anyone else she mentioned talking to. I just need answers. Once I know all the facts, maybe I can finally figure out what happened."

Nina's dark eyes assessed him for a fraction of a second. "Marcie was so nervous about testifying. That's why she called me. To give her moral support. Plus, as soon as she was done giving her testimony, we were going on a cruise."

"Did she say why she was nervous? Who she was afraid of? I'm thinking it had to be somebody besides Collier."

"Jonah Becker?"

Wyatt gave a quick nod. "That'd be my guess. It's hard to believe Collier would have the guts to do anything on his own. Did Marcie ever mention Becker to you?"

"No."

"From what she told me, most of the information she had came from overheard telephone conversations. I'm not totally convinced that her testimony would have been enough to hurt Collier, much less Becker." Wyatt watched Nina and waited.

"She used to say that Jerry Collier was *creepy*. Apparently he was always trying to cut a deal with somebody."

"Did she ever talk specifics?"

Nina shook her head. "One of the worst things she

told me she'd seen was Collier and Daniel Taabe getting into a fight."

"Right. That fight was what precipitated the investigation. It was Taabe who brought the original charges of land fraud against Jerry Collier. I talked to him today. He believes that Marcie's sympathy for the Native American cause contributed to her disappearance."

"He could be right. Marcie thought the Comanches were getting the raw end of the deal."

"Taabe's not shy about showing his resentment for the town leaders. He offered me his help in the investigation."

"Are you going to accept it?"

Wyatt shook his head. "Can't afford to. I'm afraid allowing him access to the site could become a powder keg. One tiny spark and I'd have an explosion on my hands."

Nina nodded. "Did you talk to anyone else?"

"I tried to get an interview with Billy Whitley and his wife, Charla, but they weren't available. All I know about them is that they're big friends with Tolbert and they can't stand Taabe."

"I don't know them. I never heard Marcie mention their names."

"I'm going to try and talk with them tomorrow." He paused, studying her. "So if the fight between Collier and Taabe was the worst, what did she tell you that wasn't the worst?"

Nina licked her lips. "I told you, we didn't talk about the town that much. I do remember her talking about those two men whose medical records the Ranger lab sent me."

"You mean Lattimer and Phillips, the guys who disappeared? Marcie knew them?"

"I don't know. She worked at the land office for nine years, ever since she graduated."

"What did she say about them?"

Nina looked at him thoughtfully. "It was a long time ago. But it had something to do with Native American artifacts and burial grounds, and… Oh, that was it. One of them was buying up ancient artifacts. The other one, Phillips, was the leader of the Comanche community, and the two of them came to blows over some missing artifacts."

"When was this?"

She rubbed her temple. "It was one small conversation years ago. We were celebrating something. Maybe it was when I'd just gotten my PhD."

"I'll ask Hardin about it."

"I can tell you that when the land fraud came to light, Marcie mentioned them again. She said she was afraid she'd end up disappearing, like they did."

Wyatt nodded. Marcie had told him that, too. He should have asked her who she thought was responsible for Lattimer and Phillips disappearing. "What about her and Tolbert?" he asked. "Did she think he had anything to do with those two? You still haven't told me what happened that made Marcie decide she was through with him."

"When I called to tell her I'd booked us a cruise for the week after she was supposed to testify, she said Shane had been pestering her, wanting to see her. Wanting to talk to her about the case."

"When? While she was in my custody?" Wyatt thought back. Marcie had had her cell phone, but Wyatt didn't remember hearing her talk to Shane Tolbert.

Nina shook her head. "Just before. She agreed to meet him one last time, but then when she told him she didn't want to see him again, he threatened her."

Wyatt waited.

"He told her she was his. And if he ever saw her with another man, he'd…" Her throat moved as she swallowed.

"He'd what?"

Nina's eyes widened, and she swallowed nervously. "He'd kill both of them," she whispered.

He'd expected something like that, but the words hit his ears like a stunning blow. *Kill both of them.* Was Shane Tolbert capable of killing? Had the deputy shot him?

"Wyatt?"

He blinked. "What?" He realized she'd said something.

"I said, do you think Shane shot you?"

"The bullet they pulled out of my lung was never matched to a weapon. According to the file, the Rangers tested every gun in Comanche Creek."

"Your *lung?*"

Ah, hell, he thought. That had slipped out. It sounded like a bid for sympathy.

"I thought…" She'd turned pale. Her skin looked translucent against the backdrop of that dark hair.

He didn't wait to find out what she thought. He stood. "I don't trust Tolbert, but he *was* attacked. You saw that head wound. Seven stitches isn't child's play."

"No. It's very serious."

As was her voice.

"Wyatt? I didn't show you the pictures I took, did I?"

"Which ones?"

"Of Shane's head wound."

He shook his head, but she was already up and heading through the connecting door. Within seconds she was back with her camera. "Take a look at this."

He looked at her photos of the cut on Tolbert's head. There was a red stripe, emphasized by the camera's flash, next to the bleeding laceration.

"Do you see it?" Her voice was laced with excitement and impatience.

He didn't answer. He wanted to see what she saw.

"That red streak. It's a *hesitation* wound. Can't you see it?" she asked.

"I see it." He handed the camera back to her. "I noticed it that night, but do you really think Shane conked himself on the head?"

"Do you think he stayed politely still while someone else took a practice blow?"

He had to give her that point. "You know how hard that will be to prove. The redness has already faded."

She sighed. "I know. And the inflammation of the laceration will have spread to cover it."

He nodded, then gestured toward the coffeepot. "You want some more coffee?"

She shook her head. "I'll never get to sleep if I drink any more."

He took her cup, trying to ignore the way his fingers tingled where they brushed hers. Trying to ignore how she jerked her hand away from his accidental touch.

"You said you didn't get to question Whitley?" she asked.

He set the cups down, then propped a hip on the edge of the desk. "No. I want to, though. He and his wife acted like they were furious that I'd even dare to question them. I got maybe three minutes with Mayor Sadler, most of which he spent talking. Making sure I understood just how much he does for this town." He paused. "And Trace Becker never showed up. What do you know about him?"

"Not much. Marcie called Trace a spoiled brat. She did say she wouldn't be surprised if he was in on the illegal land deal with his father and Collier." She yawned. "Excuse me. I guess I'm more tired than I realized."

"What are you planning to do in the morning?" Wyatt asked. "Go to the site or back to the lab?"

"I trust my students to handle the extraction of the bones. I want to do those scrapings of the thigh bones and send them to the Ranger lab."

"So you've got somebody to pick you up?" He was interrupted by his cell phone. It was Hardin. He answered it.

"Lieutenant? It's Reed Hardin. I just got a call from Daniel Taabe."

"Something happen?"

Nina sat up straight, her sharp gaze holding his.

"You could say that," replied Hardin. "He says he found a hatchet in the back of his pickup. A hatchet with blood on it."

"Where are you?" asked Wyatt.

"Wait. That's not all. He said he also found a bone."

"He found a bone?" Wyatt asked.

"A *bone?*" Nina echoed. "Is it my thigh bone?"

"I'm headed out to Daniel's place now." Hardin gave him directions. "I'll be right there." Wyatt hung up his phone and reached for his shoulder holster.

Nina stood. "I'm going with you."

"No, you're not." Wyatt slipped the holster on and checked his weapon.

"Yes, I am. Somebody found my missing bone, didn't they?"

Wyatt cursed under his breath. He was going to have to be a lot more careful with her around.

She headed back to her room. "I'll be ready in five minutes."

"Three, or I'm leaving." It was an empty threat, and he knew it. He reached for his windbreaker. She was right. If it was the missing thigh bone, she needed to be there. He wasn't taking any chances of contaminating the evidence. The stakes were too high—for him, for the town and for Marcie.

Chapter Eleven

Daniel Taabe lived west of Comanche Creek, in a white clapboard house with a screened porch and a tin roof. They passed a trailer park, a few large new homes set back from the road and several houses that appeared to be the same age as Taabe's.

Sheriff Hardin was already there, along with Deputy Spears. They had a big spotlight on the backseat of Taabe's truck, and Spears was crouched down, examining the floorboards with a flashlight, while Hardin stood talking to Taabe.

Wyatt parked the Jeep and got out. Out of the corner of his eye, he saw Nina heading straight for the truck.

"Lieutenant," Hardin said as Wyatt approached. He was holding a small spiral notepad and a ballpoint pen.

"Sheriff. Mr. Taabe," said Wyatt.

Daniel Taabe was frowning. His black hair was unbraided and loose. It looked damp, as if he'd just washed it.

Hardin's face was dark with worry. Wyatt couldn't blame him. If the acknowledged leader of the Native American community here was arrested, things in Comanche Creek were liable to get real ugly, real fast.

"What happened?" asked Wyatt.

Hardin pushed his hat back off his forehead. "Daniel called me about seven thirty, told me he went to get something out of his truck and noticed a small hatchet and a bone in the backseat. Says he knows they weren't there when he got home from town around lunchtime."

Wyatt nodded and waited for Hardin to offer up more information. He was certain that the hatchet was the weapon used to knock out Shane Tolbert and the bone was the one missing from the crime scene. Therefore, this discovery fell under his jurisdiction, and he had every right to march over to the truck and claim the evidence. But as much as he wanted to do that, he owed the sheriff a little courtesy.

"Kirby's checking out the truck. I see your bone collector came along." Hardin paused. Wyatt didn't speak, so he continued. "I was just asking Daniel if he saw anybody around his truck earlier."

"I was about to tell the sheriff that kids come around here all the time," said Taabe. "I hire them to do odd jobs. It keeps them busy. There were three here this afternoon, cleaning out the stables."

Hardin clicked the ballpoint pen. "Who were they?"

"Tim Hussey, Andy Jones and Kirk Foote. You wouldn't know them." Taabe's voice held a note of indignation.

"Did you see any of them hanging around your truck?" asked Wyatt.

"No. As I told the sheriff, I did not see anything."

"I take it your truck wasn't locked," Wyatt continued.

"I have no reason to lock it."

"You didn't go out to the stables while the boys were working?" asked Wyatt.

Taabe shook his head. "Of course I did. I spent

nearly two hours out there with them. I like to show them the right way to treat the horses."

Wyatt nodded. "And when they left?"

"I was still in the stables," replied Taabe. "I had a couple of mares whose hooves needed trimming."

Wyatt persisted, frustrated with Taabe's polite yet uninformative answers. "So you don't know if one or more of the boys did something to your truck."

"Yes, I do. They didn't," Taabe asserted.

Wyatt's jaw ached. "Would you mind telling me how you know?"

Taabe's mouth softened into a smile. "I'd be happy to. The stables are there, east of my house. My truck was parked where it is now, right in front of my door." He paused and lifted his head, as if sensing something. Then he pointed to the north. "I always watch the boys leave. They went north."

Wyatt leveled a gaze at him and waited.

"The only time someone could have approached my truck without me knowing was when I was inside my house, taking a shower."

"And that was when?" Hardin asked.

"Shortly after the boys left. Around five."

"You always follow the same routine?" Wyatt interjected.

Taabe smiled again. "Generally."

Wyatt turned toward the cab, checking on Nina. Spears was still searching inside the truck. Wyatt could see flashes of light as the deputy took pictures. Nina was examining the ground beside the door.

"Do you have any further questions for me?" Taabe asked. "Because I'm expecting someone."

As Wyatt stalked over to Taabe's truck, a pair of headlights appeared in the distance. He watched as they grew closer, until a white pickup pulled up several feet from where they were standing.

Ellie Penateka jumped out, dressed in faded, torn jeans and a figure-hugging yellow top. She went straight to Taabe's side and asked him what was going on.

So she was the company Daniel Taabe was expecting.

Wyatt would have liked to hear their conversation, but he needed to know what Nina had found out about the bone.

"Professor," he said, dropping to his haunches beside her.

"Yes, cowboy?" she retorted without lifting her head. Her flashlight beam played along the hard, dusty ground.

"What are you looking for?"

"Checking for prints."

"The ground looks pretty hard—" Wyatt began just as she uttered a triumphant murmur.

"There." She aimed her flashlight at a point about eighteen inches in front of her.

Wyatt saw the faint edge of what appeared to be a boot print. A large one.

"Hold this." She handed him her flashlight and retrieved a tape measure from her pocket. After placing the tape alongside the print, she snapped several photos.

"Can you get a casting of that? We could compare it with the print from the crime scene."

"I don't think so. The ground's too dusty. But we can compare the boot size. This one appears to be a size twelve." She pocketed the tape measure and pushed herself to her feet and dusted her hands together.

Size twelve. The shoe size of Tolbert, Daniel Taabe,

Deputy Spears and who knew how many others in town. With the ground that dusty, there would be no way to see any details of the boot's sole.

"What about the bone?" he asked.

Her mouth flattened, and she gave a small shake of her head.

Wyatt's pulse sped up. She'd figured something out about the bone, and she wasn't happy about it.

As if to confirm his conclusion, her fist tightened around the lanyard attached to her camera.

"I'll show you," she said and stalked toward his vehicle.

NINA HEADED TOWARD WYATT'S Jeep Liberty. She'd done her best to hang on to her professional detachment, but what she'd found in the back of Daniel Taabe's truck had her heart still pounding and her palms clammy with shock and fear.

"Deputy Spears had already photographed and bagged them," she said, reaching for the back door.

She threw the door open and stepped back.

Wyatt glanced at her sidelong. "What's wrong, Professor?" he asked as he played the flashlight beam over the bags sitting on the backseat.

She scraped her teeth over her lower lip, not trusting herself to speak.

After a few seconds of scrutiny, Wyatt bent and studied the contents of the bags. "That hatchet could match Tolbert's head wound."

Nina didn't answer.

"What's that?" Wyatt asked, zeroing in on the second bag. "That's not the missing thigh bone." A camera flash sent a dark shadow along the sharp, tense line of Wyatt's jaw.

"No, it's not."

He turned the flashlight toward her. "Nina?"

She swallowed. "It's a pelvic bone. From a female."

"A female."

For a moment neither of them spoke, but to Nina, it was as if someone were screaming into a loudspeaker.

A female pelvic bone. Was it Marcie's? Wyatt cleared his throat. "Is it from the crime scene?"

"The mud is consistent."

"You don't sound sure."

"I can't afford to jump to any conclusions." But she already had. And they terrified her. "I need to get it back to the lab and test it."

Again, the silence between them was deafening.

Finally Wyatt nodded. "And I need to take Taabe in and question him."

"You're going to arrest him? You think he attacked Shane? Why would he call the sheriff to report finding the hatchet if he's the one who attacked him?"

"Maybe he's trying to throw suspicion off himself. It's a common mistake that guilty people make."

"I don't see him as violent. He seems to be more about peace than trouble." She looked over her shoulder. Taabe was talking calmly with Sheriff Hardin. "Who's the woman? She's beautiful."

Wyatt grunted noncommittally. "Ellie Penateka. Hardin tells me she's very active in the Native American community. Apparently she's leading a petition to reclaim Comanche land in this area. She's campaigning to get a casino built here."

"She's also campaigning to get Daniel Taabe," Nina muttered.

"What do you mean?" Wyatt asked.

"Just look at them. They're trying to act as if nothing's going on, but look at that body language."

"So you're an expert on the language of the body, as well as of the skeleton?"

His voice was close to her ear—too close. She got a whiff of sharp, sweet mint, and a sense that he knew how uncomfortable he was making her.

"It doesn't take an expert to know when two people are that attracted to each other," she said. "Look how she's standing. She's completely open to him. And he's the same way. I'd bet you a month's salary they're lovers. Or if not yet, they soon will be."

"Not a bet I'm willing to take," he muttered just as a camera flash blinded her.

"What the hell?" Wyatt said, stepping away from her. "Spears, what are you doing?"

"Sorry, sir. That was an accident," replied the deputy.

Nina blinked, trying to get rid of the after-burn inside her eyelids.

"Are you done with Taabe's truck?" Wyatt asked him.

Reed Hardin walked over. "We're just about to take it in, Lieutenant. We've got a small fenced parking lot behind the office. We'll keep it there."

"Good. I'll bring Taabe in," Wyatt announced.

"You think that's necessary? He's not going anywhere," Hardin said.

Wyatt nodded. "I want to question him before he has a chance to get his story together."

Hardin sent Wyatt an odd look. "Daniel Taabe has had his story together all his life."

Nina listened to the two of them while Deputy Spears handed her the bags of evidence that he'd collected.

"Dr. Jacobson?" Spears said. "Is that everything? Do you need me to explain my notes?"

"I don't think so, Kirby. Everything appears to be pretty self-explanatory. You've got the swabs labeled and the fingerprint sheets. And it looks like you did a good job with the hatchet and the bone."

Spears seemed to swell up. "Thank you, ma'am. I mean Dr. Jacobson."

"I'll call you if I have any questions," Nina told him.

"Okay. Good." The deputy stuck his hands in his pants pockets, then pulled them out again. "Well, I need to drive Daniel's truck back to town. I'll—I'll wait to hear from you. I mean, I hope I don't. Because I hope I did everything right, but—"

"Thank you, Deputy," said Nina. "I just need your camera, so I can send the images to the Ranger lab for processing."

"Uh…" Spears sent a look toward Hardin.

"It's all right," Nina reassured him. "I'm holding the chain of custody. I'll give you a written receipt."

Spears handed the camera over to her.

"Thank you," she said to Hardin. "I'll get you copies—"

"Let's go," Wyatt snapped.

Nina jumped. He'd walked up behind her. He didn't wait for her to acknowledge that she was ready to go. He just rounded the front of the Jeep and got in the driver's seat.

She opened the passenger door. "As soon as I put the evidence bags in my kit."

"Hurry up."

She deposited the bags the deputy had given her into the metal evidence kit, and closed and locked it. Then she checked the bone and the hatchet again, telling herself she was being careful, but knowing that she might be goading Wyatt a bit. He deserved it, ordering her around like that.

Finally she closed the back door and climbed in the passenger side. She'd barely gotten her door closed and her seat belt on before he pulled away in a spray of dirt and limestone gravel.

"What is wrong with you?" she cried. "The bone could fall off the seat, the way you're driving."

"You should have secured it better."

She understood at least part of why he was agitated. She felt the same way. Ever since she'd first laid eyes on the pelvic bone, her chest had been tight with tension, and tears had been pushing closer and closer to the surface.

The bone had belonged to a *female*. And as every anthropologist knew, the pelvic bone was *the* definitive feature distinguishing male from female.

She now had a bone that could be Marcie's.

It was taking all her strength not to give in to her emotional side, so she certainly wasn't going to be drawn into his little tantrum.

After a few seconds, he muttered something.

"What?" she asked.

"I said I hate small towns."

She bit her cheek, trying not to smile and appreciating the momentary diversion. "I don't care for them, either. You can never find a decent yoga class or a really good cappuccino."

He growled.

She bit her cheek again. "What happened?"

His hands were white-knuckled on the steering wheel, and the irritation and frustration radiated from him in waves. "Sheriff Hardin didn't think it was necessary to arrest Taabe." Disgust colored his words.

"I suspect he's right. Arresting Daniel could stir up a lot of trouble in town."

Another growl.

"I take it you don't agree."

His shoulders moved in a shrug. "I don't like delays."

"Ah, yes. I recall. Or people who disagree with you." She cringed, fully expecting him to squeeze the steering wheel hard enough to break it, but to her surprise, he consciously relaxed his hands, and his jaw even quit bulging quite so much. "What's your rush to arrest Daniel Taabe? Just what do you think he will do tonight if he's not in jail? Head for the border?"

He didn't answer.

"Want to know what I think he'll be doing tonight?"

Wyatt sent her a quick, quelling glance. "No."

"I think he and Ellie Penateka—"

"I said no."

"Okay, but I guarantee you Daniel Taabe will still be here tomorrow for you to question to your heart's content. Do you want to know why?"

"No."

"Because he and Ellie are in love."

Wyatt scowled at her. "And you know that."

"I told you earlier, it's obvious in their body language. Not to mention they can't take their eyes off each other."

He frowned, as if he wanted to ask her something, but he didn't. He drove in silence, while Nina turned her attention back to the digital photos Spears had taken.

"Kirby did a good job," she said finally.

"Kirby?"

"Deputy Spears. I mean, he must have taken three shots of each drop of blood, but at least he erred on the side of thoroughness."

"What about fingerprints? Did he find any?"

"There are some, but I'll need to send them to the lab to be matched. Of course, Daniel's will be all over, and depending on how long it took him to notice the bags in the backseat, he might have smeared or destroyed any new prints."

She kept thumbing through the photos. She squinted at a close-up of the pelvic bone. Was there something odd about the bone's surface? Or was it just a trick of the light?

She opened her mouth to tell Wyatt to take her to the lab so she could get started on testing it tonight, but at that moment the last shot Kirby had taken came up.

The one he'd accidentally snapped of her and Wyatt.

Oh, no, she gasped to herself. Then she went totally still, holding her breath. Had she said that out loud? Wyatt didn't react, so she must not have.

It was a wonder that she hadn't, because what she was staring at was a photo of the two of them, and they could be a dead ringer for Taabe and Ellie.

She and Wyatt were standing close together. Wyatt's head was bent toward hers. His expression was hot, even passionate, and his posture was open, powerful, protective.

She was leaning toward him, her neck slightly arched, as if opening herself to his kiss.

That wasn't what they'd been doing, but judging by the picture, it could have been.

What she'd told him about Taabe and Ellie echoed in her brain. *I'd bet you a month's salary they're lovers. Or if not yet, they soon will be.* She moaned silently.

"What?"

She jumped. "I didn't say anything."

"Yes, you did."

She turned off the camera. "Take me to the lab at the college."

"No. It's too late."

"I want to look at this bone. There's something odd about it."

"Tomorrow."

"Hey, cowboy, you're the one who said you didn't like delays."

He turned onto the road that led to the Bluebonnet Inn. "And you pointed out that I don't like people who disagree with me. So why do you keep doing it?"

"To irritate you?" she snapped.

"That would be my guess," he shot back.

She looked at her watch. "It's only... Oh."

"It's only what time?"

She bit her lip. "Almost midnight."

"Right. Still want to start a whole new set of tests?"

"Actually, yes. I don't have to tell you what it means that this pelvis is from a female."

"Are you positive that it came from the crime scene?"

She glared at his profile. "It's a bone, it's got mud smeared all over it and it showed up with a bloody hatchet that matches Shane's description of the weapon in his attack."

Wyatt stopped the Jeep in front of the inn and killed the engine. He turned and gazed at her steadily.

"Okay. I can't say for certain, not without the tests. Which is why I want to go to the lab." She tried to suppress a yawn but wasn't successful.

"See? You can't start all that testing tonight. You're exhausted. You'd probably screw up the tests. I need to take you upstairs and put you to bed."

He looked at her, his blue eyes twinkling, and a hot

thrill coursed through her at the idea of him lifting her in his arms and carrying her upstairs like Rhett Butler.

She swallowed, and the twinkle in his eyes faded, replaced by an intensity she hadn't seen before—not even when he was ready to throttle Sheriff Hardin for refusing to arrest Taabe.

He looked like…

She swallowed. He looked like he did in the photo. Hot, powerful, passionate.

Something caught and started to burn deep inside her. She lifted her chin just slightly. For an indefinable time they stared at each other.

Then Wyatt blinked and opened the driver's-side door.

"Tomorrow," he said gruffly.

Chapter Twelve

By the time Nina was ready for bed, she could barely
hold her eyes open. She yawned and looked longingly
at the turned-down covers. But her brain was still
churning.

She had so much evidence and so few answers. And
now a female pelvic bone had been added to the mix.

If it was Marcie's...

She couldn't go there. Just like Wyatt had reminded
her, nothing was certain until she had the test results.

Test results. Her gaze snapped to her laptop. She
needed to check her e-mail in case the forensics lab had
sent her the results of the DNA comparison of the hair
found at the crime scene.

Within a few seconds she was watching, her heart in
her throat, as her new messages downloaded.

And there it was. Sender? The Ranger Forensics lab.

It was short. No wasted words. Attached please
find...

Nina opened the attachment and scanned it
quickly. Professional and to the point, and precisely
what she'd expected.

She'd written several reports just like this, without
once thinking about the real, grieving people on the re-

ceiving end of the information. Never again, though. She would never be able to stare at a set of remains again without remembering the grief that flooded her heart this minute.

Or the sense of loneliness.

A tear slid from her eye and rolled down her cheek. She wasn't a forensic anthropologist—not right now. She was a grieving friend. A quick swipe with her fingers got rid of the tear, but not the weight of sadness.

She turned and looked at the closed door that separated her from Wyatt, worrying her lower lip with her teeth. She needed to tell him; he needed to know.

It was as important to him as it was to her. Maybe more. After all, he was responsible.

Wasn't he? As much as Nina needed someone to blame, the longer she knew Wyatt, the harder it was to blame him.

She knocked on the door between their rooms. When he didn't answer right away, she was afraid he'd already gone to sleep. Should she wake him? She knocked again, lightly, then turned the knob, fully expecting the room to be dark.

But the soft glow of the bedside lamp lit the room— the empty room.

Too late, Nina recognized the warm scent of steam and bleached towels and soap.

She needed to get out of here—now.

Then the bathroom door opened, and there he was, right in front of her, dressed in nothing but briefs, with a towel hanging from one hand.

He was scowling, but as soon as his gaze met hers, his expression changed. "What's the matter, Professor? You okay?"

"I shouldn't have…" Nina stumbled over her words. "It can wait." She took a step backward.

"Hang on!" He grabbed the pair of sweatpants that were slung over the back of a chair and pulled them on. Then in one stride, he was at her side. "Now, what is it? Did you hear something? Has someone been in your room again?"

She shook her head. "I—I just checked my e-mail. The results are back on the hair."

"Yeah?"

Nina heard the fear and anticipation in his voice. He was as anxious to know the results as she had been.

And he'd be just as devastated.

She took a deep breath, filled with the odor of fresh clean skin and soap. She scraped her lower lip with her teeth and felt cool air on her cheek as another tear spilled over. "The DNA from the hair was a match with Marcie's. No question."

His gaze narrowed. After an instant of unnatural stillness, he brushed his fingers tenderly across her cheek. The slight touch sent a sweet, sad ache through her.

"We expected that," he murmured.

She squeezed her eyelids shut, trying to stop any more tears. Of course, it did no good. "I know," she whispered. "It's just hard."

"Yeah. It is." He pulled her close, cradling the back of her head in his palm.

She pressed her face into the hollow between his neck and shoulder, where his skin was warm and damp. Beneath its silky surface, his firm, vibrant muscles rippled, and his chest rose and fell with his strong, steady breathing. She slid her arms around his waist, just to absorb more of the comfort he offered her.

She missed Marcie.

"Something in me never let her go," she whispered. "I believed she was out there somewhere. That she was waiting for something—waiting until she felt safe enough to come back."

He pressed his cheek against her hair. "Are you okay?" he asked.

"Yes. I am." She laughed quietly. "I don't know why I'm acting like this."

"You've got a right."

She hugged him tighter, pressing her nose into his damp flesh, breathing deeply. His closeness and scent were comforting, she told herself. Her insides were warm and glowing from his gentle embrace and their shared sadness—not hot and liquid because she craved the taste of him on her tongue.

He pressed a kiss to the top of her head, a sweet, protective gesture at odds with the quick, staccato beat of his heart.

Her own pulse sped up, and her breasts, already taut and full where they pressed against his chest, suddenly grew ultrasensitive.

She pulled away.

His hand slid from the back of her head to her neck, and his thumb brushed across the line of her jaw gently, caressingly. "Do you want to leave?"

She shook her head, not knowing if she was answering him or wishing he would stop talking. The way she was feeling right now couldn't be described in words.

Words only complicated everything.

He nodded, as if he knew what she was thinking and agreed. She felt the movement of his head against her hair. Before he could speak, she pressed her fingers against his lips.

To her surprise, he opened his mouth and slid his tongue along her fingertips. She gasped.

He lowered his head, pushing her own fingers to her mouth, sending even more heat to her core. She slid her hand around to his nape, where his hair was damp and tousled, and pulled his head closer.

And accepted his kiss.

When their lips touched, he sighed—a ragged expulsion of breath. Hesitating, he hovered there, the full center of his lower lip barely grazing hers.

Without thinking about the consequences, she ran her tongue over the seam that linked their lips.

With a gasp, he let his mouth cover hers, and their tongues met. He tasted just like she knew he would. Hot and sweet and minty, with an undercurrent of something dark and delicious.

Then his hands were around her back and pulling her to him. The thin silk of her camisole seemed to melt as he imprinted his body on hers. Her nipples tightened until they ached. Her thigh muscles contracted reflexively, responding to the rising heat his touch was coaxing from her sexual center.

Wyatt tore his mouth away and studied her face, his eyes as hot and blue as a flame of pure oxygen. "Professor? I don't want to take advantage—"

Her fingers curled into fists. "You're not," she grated.

"You sure about this?"

She couldn't answer. She had no breath. All she could do was kiss him again, more deeply.

That was all the answer Wyatt needed. He picked her up and laid her down on the bed, then lowered himself beside her. It was all he could do not to rip away the delicate material of her panties and camisole.

But he restrained himself. Instead, he caressed her

bare skin, feeling her abs and thigh muscles contract when his teasing fingers touched them. He slid his fingers under the thin band of elastic and inched her panties lower and lower.

His immediate goal was to savor every second of this fantasy—this small moment out of time.

Neither one of them was exactly rational right now. Especially not Nina. She was grieving for her friend. Seeking comfort.

Later, when she was thinking clearly, he knew for a fact that she'd regret this momentary lapse of reason. But he wiped that thought from his head. If this was the only chance he ever got to act on the longings she'd generated in him from the first time he'd met her, he'd take it.

Every second of it.

The first time he'd laid eyes on her two years ago, he'd wanted to sink his fingers into her thick dark hair and watch it slide like black silk across his skin.

He'd wanted to skim his tongue across every inch of her creamy, petal-soft skin. If her face and the tops of her breasts were that creamy and smooth, what would the softer skin of her tummy feel like?

And the protected, sensitive skin of her inner thighs?

And the even softer, erotically charged skin of…

His hardness throbbed as her hands, busy pushing his sweatpants down, brushed it.

"Keep going," he breathed as he pushed the black satiny camisole up. Her belly and abs were as taut and shapely as they'd felt under his fingertips. He brushed his palms across the underside of her breasts. She moaned aloud and shoved his sweatpants farther down.

He kicked them off.

Then he sat up and brought her with him, holding

her so he could tongue her nipples. She arched, giving him easier access, and in one sleek movement, wrapped her legs around his waist.

She raised her arms so he could yank off her camisole. Her breasts were beautiful, perfectly shaped—perfectly sized. Not small, yet not too big. He could spend eternity there, touching, tasting, savoring.

But Nina wanted more. Without saying a word, she let him know that she was ready. She tightened her legs. She threw back her head and moaned as he feasted on one creamy globe and then the other.

And finally, she fisted her hands in his hair and forced him to look up into her eyes.

"Now," she said, holding his gaze. "Now."

He laid her down and raised himself above her. "I don't want to do something you're not ready for—" he began, but she stopped his words with her fingers.

He thrust, and she took him in.

He gasped aloud as her heat enveloped him. She was so tight, so hot, so perfect. He sank hilt-deep, hearing the hitch in her breathing as he began to move.

She ran her fingers down his shoulders to caress his biceps, then back up, as she met him thrust for thrust, matching his rhythm. And the whole time she watched him. Her gaze never wavered.

Wyatt moved slowly, taunting them both with long strokes that brought him closer and closer to losing control.

Each time he moved, she moaned, low and breathy, and moved to match his rhythm.

After an indefinable time, he felt his muscles tense, felt the sweet, hot fire that signaled his coming release. He slowed down. "Let's take it easy," he hissed softly.

Nina shook her head. "No. Let's take it hard."

Matching words to deed, she ground against him, pushing him, demanding more, until he couldn't hold back for another second.

Then the fire ignited and spread. At the same time, he felt the change in her. The catch in her breathing, the tiny contractions, which told him she was as close as he was. So he pumped up the rhythm and made sure they came together.

NINA AWOKE TO SUNLIGHT streaming in through the window and the rhythmic sounds of Wyatt's long, smooth breaths. He was on his back, with the sheet angled across the edge of his hip.

She was curled up on her side, and for a while, she just lay there and watched him breathe. His brown hair was tousled, softening his features and making him look innocent and young.

His mouth was curved in a slight smile. The eyelashes, which were barely darker than his hair, lay against his cheek like fringes, hiding the intense blue of his eyes.

She traced the line of his jaw to the cleft in his chin with her gaze. Then down the elegant line of his neck to his chest.

There, below his right collarbone, was a scar. An ugly, jaggedly curved scar that disappeared under his arm.

Where he'd been shot. Where they'd cut the bullet out of his lung. Her throat contracted until she could hardly breathe.

She'd been shocked when he said he'd been shot in the lung. She'd thought the bullet had hit his shoulder, and nobody had ever told her any differently.

When they'd taken him away on a stretcher, with the

EMTs shouting commands and hustling everybody out of the way, she'd been resentful at so much hoopla over a shoulder wound. Tough guys on TV still chased villains after being shot in the shoulder.

Meanwhile, whoever had shot him had disappeared into thin air, with her best friend as his captive.

She'd yelled at Wyatt as they rolled the stretcher past her. She remembered her exact words.

My best friend is gone. She could be dead, and it's all your fault.

"I'm so sorry," she whispered silently as her gaze traced every inch, every millimeter of damaged skin. It shone pale against his tanned flesh, like the silver star he wore pinned to his shirt. And like the Ranger badge, the scar was a symbol of his courage.

He'd taken a bullet to his lung trying to save Marcie. He could have died.

Her breath caught in a near sob. How could she have been so wrong about him?

Each and every person who became a Texas Ranger took an oath to protect not only the state of Texas and their fellow Rangers but any innocent person.

These were men of legend. Heroes.

Heroes. She nodded to herself and sighed. How wonderful to be the recipient of such protection, such courage, such caring.

If she were looking for a hero, she could certainly do worse than Wyatt Colter. Against her better judgment, almost against her will, she reached out to touch the scar. Her fingers hovered over his skin, trembling with emotion.

They'd made love last night, more than once. If the fact that she was in his bed wasn't proof that it hadn't been a dream, the soreness between her thighs was.

Many people would say that what they'd done was

the ultimate intimacy. That nothing could bring two people closer together.

But right now, her desire to touch his scar, to feel the place where the deadly bullet had entered his flesh, felt much more intimate.

She slid her gaze from the tip of her finger to the curve of his scar, then up to his face—and met his sleepy gaze. "Oh!" she gasped.

He caught her hand in his. "Good morning," he muttered without taking his eyes off her. He stared at her as heat rose in his eyes. Then slowly he pressed her fingers to his chest.

To the rough, damaged skin of his scar.

Tears welled in her eyes. Embarrassment? Maybe. An awful ache at the pain he'd felt? Certainly.

"I'm sorry," she said.

The heat in his gaze flickered and changed to blue ice. He took his hand away. "Why? You didn't wake me."

"N-No," she stammered. "I meant—"

"It's getting late." He threw back the covers and got up, reaching for his clothes.

His brusque dismissal sent chills up her spine. She opened her mouth to say…what? She had no idea.

He headed for the bathroom, his clothes in his hand. A couple of seconds later, the pipes creaked. He'd turned on the shower.

She lay there staring at the closed bathroom door. Why had he deliberately pressed her hand against his chest—against his scar—and then acted as though he didn't know what she was apologizing for.

Then it hit her. He did know what she'd meant.

He hadn't misunderstood her apology; he'd rejected it. Oh, she'd made a big mistake. She should have known better. She'd never been cut out for casual relationships.

She knew—because she'd tried them before. But her idea of a relationship included trust and safety. And in her experience, casual was the antithesis of safety.

Quickly, she scanned the floor for her panties and camisole, but she didn't see them. Feeling around in the rumpled sheets, she finally came up with them.

By the time she had slipped them on and was ready to dart through the connecting door and back to her own room, Wyatt had appeared from the bathroom. He'd showered and put on dress khakis, but he hadn't shaved. His hair was still wet, and his chest and abs were damp.

She kicked the sheets away from her legs. "I've got to shower, too," she mumbled just as a knock sounded on the door. She froze, then pulled the sheets up again.

Wyatt reached for his holster, slung over the back of the desk chair.

"Lieutenant?" Betty Alice's cheerful voice cut the air like a paring knife. She knocked again.

Nina stared at Wyatt, who frowned and held a finger up to his lips.

She shook her head and pointed toward the connecting door, silently asking for a couple of seconds to escape into her own room, but he ignored her plea.

He opened the door, swinging it wide, toward the bed. If Betty Alice didn't come all the way into the room, she wouldn't see Nina.

Why it mattered to her what Betty Alice saw or didn't see, Nina couldn't say. Maybe because of the smirk on the woman's face when Nina had refused to change rooms. Or when she'd declined the offer of a lock on the connecting door.

Her face burned. She should have let Betty Alice install that lock.

"I found this on the desk this morning when I opened up," Betty Alice was telling Wyatt. "When I saw what the envelope said, I thought I'd better bring it right up to you."

"Did you see who brought it?" he asked.

"Why, no, I didn't. I got up about an hour ago to start my cinnamon loaf. It must have been before that, because I can hear the door from my kitchen, but not from my bedroom."

"Do you leave the front door unlocked?"

Betty Alice laughed. "No, but probably half the people in town know where the spare key is—under the doormat. This is a friendly town, for the most part. Anybody can get in if they really want to."

"Thanks."

Nina heard the dismissive tone in Wyatt's voice. Apparently Betty Alice didn't.

"Well? Aren't you going to see what it says?" she asked.

"I appreciate you bringing it up to me."

There was a pause of a few seconds. Then, "Well, I guess I'd better be getting downstairs. My cinnamon loaf needs to come out of the oven."

Wyatt closed the door. He didn't budge, and Nina held her breath until Betty Alice's footsteps faded down the hardwood stairs.

Finally, he looked at the note in his hand and then at Nina.

She got the message. She was dismissed, just as Betty Alice had been. He wanted to read his note in private. She ducked her head. "It won't take me long to shower and dress. If you don't mind running me out to the site, I'll catch a ride back to the lab with one of my students." She jumped up and sprang toward the connecting door.

"Wait."

She turned her head, feeling naked in her black camisole and bikini panties.

Wyatt had crossed to the writing desk and picked up an ornate letter opener. "It's addressed to you, too. Lieutenant Colter and Dr. Jacobson." He held it up to show her.

She got a glimpse of plain block letters before he slit the top of the envelope. He shook the folded sheet of paper out onto the desk and used a pen and the letter opener to ease it open.

Nina took a couple of wary steps toward him, still feeling viciously exposed in her underwear. As he opened up the note, she spotted another piece of paper inside.

His eyes scanned the sheet of paper, and he cursed. Then cursed again as he used the letter opener to flip over the enclosed rectangle. As she watched, his brows shot up and his face drained of color.

"What is it? Wyatt?"

"Damn it!" he growled. "Can you lift prints off paper?"

"Sure," she said. She was beginning to get scared. Wyatt looked as if he'd seen a ghost. "The lab at the community college has the necessary chemicals. What does the note say?"

"It says, 'I'll contact you about this in a few days.'"

"About what?"

Wyatt's gaze met hers. His eyes looked somehow hot and icy at the same time. His jaw muscles bulged.

"Wyatt?"

"This," he bit out. "Take a look."

She stepped over to the desk. There, looking dark

against the white of the note paper, was a photograph. Nina stared in disbelief. Her heart raced so fast, she felt like she couldn't take a breath. "Dear heavens," she whispered. It took a moment before she could say anything else. "Is that the date stamp?" She pointed to the right lower corner of the photograph.

"Yeah. It's dated the first of this month." Wyatt's voice was void of emotion.

Nina squinted. "This *year?*"

He didn't answer, but he didn't have to. She knew it was.

She intertwined her fingers together and pressed the knuckles against her mouth. A slightly hysterical chuckle escaped her lips. "So I'm not crazy?"

"If you are, then I am, too."

"You see what I see? A picture of…" Her voice died. She swallowed and tried again. "Of Marcie, date stamped a week ago."

She stood there, her mouth dry as a bone as Wyatt met her gaze. Then she said, "That means Marcie's alive."

Chapter Thirteen

Nina stared at the photograph of her best friend. "Who could have sent this? Marcie's kidnapper?"

Wyatt didn't speak. He looked as stunned as she felt.

"Do you think it's a fake? That date could have been added in a computer program."

He nodded.

Neither one of them spoke for a few seconds. Then Wyatt said, "Get your kit."

She was already at the door. She popped into her room, grabbed her forensics kit and her camera and hurried back without even stopping to put on a robe.

She took several shots of the note and photo, then pulled on gloves and bagged the note and the photo.

"Get dressed. I want to get this tested for fingerprints now," Wyatt told her.

She locked the evidence bag in her kit and headed back to her room. By the time she'd showered and dressed, Wyatt was gone. So she hurried downstairs.

He was standing near the foot of the stairs, with a cup of coffee in his hand, scrutinizing the front desk and lobby as if he could force them to yield up the secret of who had delivered the envelope.

He turned and held up his cup as she stepped off the last step.

She shook her head. "No. I'm ready to figure out what's going on here."

He nodded in agreement. "I just got a call from the sheriff. The footprint castings revealed a size twelve boot with an indentation on the right rear of the heel."

"Does he have a match?"

"He said Tolbert and Spears both wear a twelve, as do Trace Becker and Daniel Taabe."

"So either of the deputies could have left that print."

"Or Becker, snooping around. This brings into question Taabe's claim about the bone and hatchet left in his truck, too. That boot print you photographed could have been his own."

"What about our fingerprint? Should we try to lift it here at the college or take it to Austin?"

He set his cup on the desk and headed for the door. "Is there an advantage to driving for an hour to get to the Ranger lab?"

"For a possible fingerprint ID, probably none, unless you'd rather have someone other than me do the matching."

"I want it fast. If that picture is real…" He stopped, and Nina knew his brain was whirling with all the implications, just like hers was.

"Then Marcie's alive," she said, her voice quavering. "And either she or her kidnapper sent this picture to us."

Wyatt climbed in the Jeep and started the engine, while Nina stowed her forensics kit in the backseat and got in on the passenger side. She was thoughtful as Wyatt backed out of the parking space.

Marcie was *alive*. But that wasn't the most shocking thing.

For two years, Nina had prayed that her friend was still alive, but in all that time, she'd never considered the consequences.

If Marcie really was alive, then she'd faked her death, and worse…

"Wyatt, do you think it was Marcie who shot you?"

Wyatt grimaced to himself as he deliberately loosened his fingers from the steering wheel and put the vehicle in gear. Nina's mind was fitting the pieces together exactly the same way his was.

And both of them were venturing into dangerous territory.

"Professor, our job is to get the facts—not speculate."

Nina's breath whooshed out in a sigh. "You're right. I know. But I can't stop thinking about it, trying to figure it out. Because if Marcie's not dead, then…" He knew where she was headed. "Then we've got a third body. A female."

He heard in her voice how close she was to falling apart. Again, he knew how she felt. And again, he had to rein her in for her own sake. "You've got to stay calm. Stay rational. Hopefully we'll have an answer soon. If there's a fingerprint on the paper or the photo, you'll lift it. The Ranger database has the prints of just about everyone in Comanche Creek."

"But if the photo's a fake—"

"You're going to test the DNA from the pelvic bone. One way or another, the facts will give us the answer."

"The facts."

Her voice was steadier now. He'd managed to tap into her rational brain and stop her imagination from spiraling out of control.

Now if only he could stop his.

"How likely is it that you can get a print from the paper?" Maybe if he could get her to talk about facts and science, it would help him to stop rehashing all the ways he could have prevented Marcie from being kidnapped.

"Lifting prints from paper is dicey at best," she said.

He could tell by the tone of her voice that he'd successfully distracted her.

She went on. "The note was written on copy paper, which is relatively smooth compared to bond. And because of its acid content, it should hold the print well. But any ordinary TV buff should know to use gloves to handle a note. So I don't hold out much hope. The photo may be a different story. Glossy photo paper is an excellent medium for prints."

"Yeah," he commented. "I've ruined a few photos by touching them before the ink was completely dry."

She didn't respond to his effort at conversation. He glanced sidelong at her and saw that she was deep in thought.

He just hoped she was mulling over the best way to lift any fingerprints she found, rather than asking herself which scenario was worse—that her best friend had let her think she was dead, or that she'd been in the clutches of a kidnapper for two years.

AN HOUR LATER at the community college lab, Wyatt closed the door behind the courier. "Okay. The courier is on his way to the Ranger lab with the scrapings from the pelvic bone."

"Good," Nina said distractedly. She turned the head of the lighted magnifying lamp a fraction of an inch. *There. Finally. A decent print.* She straightened with a groan. "I think I've found one."

Wyatt stalked over and stood behind her chair as he peered through the large magnifying lens. "Where is it?" He bent to get a good look at her handiwork.

"On the back of the photo. I couldn't find one decent partial on the paper. And this is the only one on the photo."

"Good job." He put his hand on her shoulder, surprising her.

And thrilling her. And not just because of that moment, she remembered their wild night of lovemaking. Thrilling her in a way she'd never felt before.

Even after last night, she was surprised that he would cross the line between professional and personal with even that small gesture of a hand on her shoulder. He was so steeped in the responsibility of his position as a Texas Ranger.

She had to be careful, though. Even if he was a Ranger, he was still a man. She knew nothing about him.

Until last night all he'd been to her was the man who had let her friend die.

As far as she knew, for him their night together had been no more than a way to pass the time until this investigation was over and he could go back to his life and she to hers.

"Professor? Dazzle me with your knowledge."

"Right." She blinked and forced her brain back to the job at hand. "The photo was printed on a home photo printer, using standard four-inch-by-six-inch glossy photo paper. The glossy side can yield a print of lab quality. Like you said, getting a fingerprint on a photo can ruin it. But what people don't know is that even the back side of glossy paper is slick enough to take a great print."

"And that's where you found this one?"

"Here. Take a look." She slid her chair a little sideways so he could look through the magnifying lamp at the back of the photo. When he bent his head, his hair brushed her cheek.

She swallowed, doing her best to ignore the mint on his breath, the heat that radiated from his body and her instantaneous response to his closeness.

"Wow," he muttered. "It's almost a complete print."

Her heart swelled with pride. "Wow" was a supreme compliment, coming from him. "He probably left it while he was putting the paper in the printer. He was super careful about touching the front but didn't think about the back."

"Well, it's a beauty."

"I've still got to lift it." She pushed the magnifying lamp out of the way, thinking Wyatt would move away, but he didn't. Nor did he remove his hand. "I need room," she said reluctantly, quashing the urge to tilt her head and press her chin against his fingers. "This isn't going to be easy."

He straightened and gave her shoulder a squeeze before removing his hand.

She took a sheet of fingerprint film and peeled off the protective paper, and slowly and deliberately applied the sticky film to the back of the photo. Then lifted the fingerprint.

She held the clear film up to the light. "I got it," she whispered.

"Okay," Wyatt said, excitement evident in his voice. "Let's get it scanned in and compare it with the database."

Within a few minutes, Nina had uploaded the fingerprint to the Ranger database in Austin.

Wyatt made a quick call to the lab. "Liz said it will probably take a few hours to run through all the fingerprints," he told Nina a few minutes later. "I let her know the scrapings were coming in and told her to run them specifically against Marcie's DNA." He assessed her. "I'm betting you haven't eaten, and I know you didn't get much sleep last night."

She felt her face heat up. Of course he knew. He was there. He was the reason she hadn't slept. And neither had he. She grabbed the fingerprint sheet out of the scanner and placed it in a file folder. It was something to do until the heat in her cheeks dissipated.

"So you want to get some lunch?" he asked. "Then I'll take you back to the inn so you can take a nap. Liz promised to call me when the run finishes."

She looked at her watch. "I was hoping Todd would have some bones for me to look at by now."

As if on cue, the door to the lab opened and Todd backed in, carrying a large crate. "Guess what, Dr. Jacobson?" he panted as he set the crate gingerly on the lab table.

"You found more remains," said Nina.

Todd beamed. "Not just remains. Skulls. At least parts of skulls."

Nina's heart jumped. "Skulls? How many?"

Todd shook his head. "I'm not sure. They're mostly in fragments. But there are a few large pieces, and one really nice specimen. Mandible, maxilla, and zygomatic…all intact, with teeth."

"What the hell does that mean?" Wyatt broke in.

Nina grinned at him. "Basically it means jaw, chin and cheekbones."

"That sounds good," Wyatt replied.

"It's great. The teeth could provide a definite ID." She turned back to Todd. "But you couldn't possibly have found nothing but skull fragments."

Todd beamed again. "There's a lot more coming, but I knew you'd want the skulls first."

"Get it all in here, and get Julie to come help us," said Nina. "We need to match bones to bones so we can figure out how many sets of remains we have here. We're going to need more tables."

She met Wyatt's eyes and knew he was on the same page as she was. Maybe with all the bone fragments Todd and Julie had unearthed, she could finally get a handle on just how many sets of remains had been dumped into that shallow grave.

And whether any of them belonged to Marcie.

Wyatt inclined his head. "So I'm guessing you'll be busy here for a while," he said.

She nodded, her mind already on the contents of the crate Todd was opening.

"Okay, then," said Wyatt. "The mayor's assistant has some appointments lined up for me this afternoon. Maybe I can finish interviewing everyone. I'll be back here by three-thirty or four. We can get something to eat. Okay?"

Nina watched as Todd lifted the partially intact skull out of the crate. It was still covered with dirt and mud, but Todd was right. It was a beautiful specimen.

"Set it over there, and let's get started cleaning it up." She pointed at an empty table, then looked around. "Wyatt? Did you say three-thirty?"

But he was gone.

BILLY WHITLEY CURSED AND let the front legs of his straight-backed chair drop against the hardwood floor of the mayor's conference room with a thud. "That is a damn lie," he barked. "Get my wife in here. She'll tell you."

Wyatt eyed the man narrowly. He didn't like him.

Not one bit. Of course, that shouldn't make a difference. Facts were facts. Evidence was evidence. Personalities shouldn't factor in.

"Marcie James stated in her sworn deposition that you accepted money to alter certain documents you had access to as the county clerk. Are you saying Marcie lied under oath?"

Billy slapped his breast pocket. He was either a smoker or an ex-smoker, and the gesture was a clear indicator to Wyatt that he was nervous about something. "Are you saying I'm lying now?"

Wyatt pushed a photocopy of Marcie's deposition across the table. "Just going by the facts. Here's her statement. It's highlighted right there."

"I can't believe it." Billy shook his head rapidly as he pushed the paper back toward Wyatt. "She was a sweet girl. I don't know why she'd tell tales like that."

Wyatt didn't touch the paper and didn't comment. He just sat quietly in the worn leather executive chair. The mayor's conference room furniture was a lot like the mayor himself. Over fifty years old, polished and yet rough at the same time, and for the most part, welcoming.

Finally, Billy looked up at him from under his brows. "Did she say she had proof?"

Wyatt stayed still.

"Because if she did, I'd like to see it. I can refute it. I didn't do anything." His upper lip glistened with sweat. "Somebody's trying to frame me."

Wyatt sat up, feigning interest. "Yeah? Who would that be?"

"I don't know. I don't have any enemies."

Wyatt sincerely doubted that. "Marcie also said you threatened her."

"Now, you listen to me. Ask anyone in town. Marcie was flighty…" Billy actually looked around, as if someone might be listening. "Know what I mean?"

"No. Actually I don't. Explain it to me."

"I was her boss. So naturally, if she did something wrong, I had to let her know, right? Well, she didn't take that too well. She'd cry if I asked her to retype something or find a misfiled deed." He shifted in his chair. "Why, one time she…" He stopped, looked nervous.

"She what?"

"Nothing."

"Who else has access to the documents in your office?"

"Now, see, there's what I don't understand. You keep accusing me of altering documents, but I haven't seen anything. You got the documents?"

He had Wyatt there. All Wyatt had was Marcie's deposition. She'd claimed she made copies of the altered documents and put them in a safe-deposit box, but after she disappeared, the documents were nowhere to be found.

"That's all for now, Mr. Whitley. Don't leave town without notifying me. We're not done here."

Billy shot up out of the chair as if it had burned him.

"Hold it." Wyatt stood, too. He pressed the intercom button for Mayor Sadler's assistant.

"Yes?"

It was Charla Whitley. Billy's wife. Wyatt had been dismayed to find out that she was an administrative assistant to the mayor. This case was definitely a tangled web.

"Where's Helen?" Wyatt asked.

"She went for coffee." Charla's voice was hostile, even over the intercom. "Anything I can do for you?"

"Yes. Please come in here," said Wyatt.

"But…Billy hasn't come out yet," Charla hedged.

At that instant, Billy turned and headed for the door.

Chapter Fourteen

"I said hold it, Whitley."

Billy froze.

"That's right, Mrs. Whitley. He hasn't come out yet. Please come in."

Within about seven seconds the door opened, and Charla Whitley stomped in, glaring at Billy. They'd obviously made plans to talk between interviews, to keep their answers consistent. But Wyatt wasn't about to give them even one second alone together.

"Please have a seat, Mrs. Whitley," said Wyatt. He turned to Billy. "You can leave."

Charla huffed, but she sat.

Billy stared at the back of her head for a few seconds, then walked out the door.

"Close it," Wyatt called.

The door slammed.

"You're not making any friends here," Charla commented, aiming her glare at him.

"Not my intent," he said. "My job is to figure out whose remains are in that shallow grave and who put them there."

Charla crossed her arms.

"How long have you worked for the mayor?"

"About five years."

"Did you know Mason Lattimer and Ray Phillips?" She didn't react, but he saw her dark eyes flicker.

"Lattimer was an antiques broker who was rumored to be buying up Native American artifacts from Trace Becker. Phillips was—"

"I know Ray."

"You *know* him? When was the last time you talked to him?"

"I don't remember. Maybe last year."

Wyatt's brows rose. "Yeah? Can you prove it?"

A smirk lit her face. "Why should I have to?"

"It would save us a lot of time if we could rule him out as one of the bodies at the crime scene."

Charla grimaced. "What makes you think he might be dead?"

Wyatt shuffled through the thick folder in front of him. It was all the evidence and papers connected with the land fraud deal and Marcie's disappearance. "The last record of anyone seeing him alive was over three years ago. And it's been that long since any of his credit cards were used. He also hasn't paid taxes, and his disability checks have been stacking up at his post office box."

As he listed the reasons, Charla's mouth seemed to grow tighter and tighter.

"Something wrong?" he asked.

She shook her head stiffly. "Ray was…a friend of mine. A *good* friend."

"So now you're saying *was?* Has it really been only a year since you talked to him? Where was he? What was he doing?"

"Maybe it was longer." She met his gaze, and her black eyes narrowed. "Time flies."

He asked her a few more questions, mostly about Billy and his dealings on the city council, but she was as indignant as her husband had been that anyone would accuse him of wrongdoing. So he dismissed her.

He'd expected her reaction to his questions about her husband. But she'd surprised him about Ray Phillips. She'd seemed really upset when she heard the news that he hadn't used his cards and hadn't cashed his checks in over three years. Wyatt was glad he'd already seized the contents of Phillips's post office box.

The intercom buzzed. "Lieutenant, Sheriff Hardin is on line one. Will you be interviewing anyone else this afternoon? Charla was the last interview I have on my schedule."

"No. No one else. Thanks, Helen." He picked up the phone. "Hardin? What's up?"

"I've got a boy in my office who says he saw someone heading out toward Daniel's house around the time we figure the hatchet and bone were planted," Hardin said. "You want to be here while I question him? He's about twelve and so scared he's about to…you know."

"I'll be right there."

As he hung up, Wyatt glanced at his watch. *After four. Damn. He'd promised Nina he'd be at the lab by now.* He called her as he headed next door to the sheriff's office. The phone rang four times.

"Yes?" Her voice sounded irritated and preoccupied at the same time.

"Busy?" Wyatt couldn't suppress a smile at her tone.

"Very."

"I'm not going to make it by four o'clock."

"That's fine, because I'm not nearly finished."

"I'm headed over to the sheriff's office to talk to

a kid who might have seen something at Taabe's house."

"Who? One of the kids who was helping Daniel in his stables?"

"No idea. Hardin didn't give me a name. Are your students there?"

"They're washing bones as we speak."

"Well, make sure they stick around until I get there. I'm sure this won't take more than an hour, hour and a half at the most."

"Uh-huh," she replied absently.

"Those must be some interesting bones you're looking at."

She laughed, and the sound of it shot straight through him right down to his groin. "You have no idea."

"Okay, I'll see you around five-thirty or six. Nina, stay there. Lock the doors. And make the students stay there with you." He started to say goodbye and then thought of one more safety measure. "In fact, let me talk to Todd. I'll tell him to stay—"

But Nina had already hung up.

As he entered the sheriff's office, Wyatt dialed the Ranger lab. "Lizzie, what's going on up there with that print I sent you? I thought I'd hear back from you hours ago. And the courier delivered the bone scrapings, right?"

"We got them. Sorry, Wyatt. The computer's been down. The IT guys kept promising *one more hour.* That fingerprint you sent came up around two-thirty, so the prints are running now. I'll call you as soon as I get a match. The scrapings will probably be tomorrow at the earliest. You can't imagine how backed up we are."

"Can you check with the captain? I need that info ASAP."

"He already told us to make it a priority."

"You're the best, Liz."

"I know," she answered with a smile in her voice.

When he got to Hardin's office, the sheriff waved him in. On the other side of the desk, in a straight-backed chair, with his hands clasped in his lap and his bare feet barely touching the floor, was a Native American boy of about thirteen.

His complexion was as ruddy as Taabe's, and his hair and eyes as black. He was holding an MP3 player. The white wire led up to the earbuds in his ears.

Choosing a side chair where he had a good view of both of them, Wyatt sat. He was close enough to the kid that he could intimidate him if he leaned forward. He doubted he'd have to, though. For all his posturing with the music player, the boy looked terrified.

"Kirk, we're ready to get started now," Hardin said.

Kirk ducked his head and took the earbuds out. As he wrapped the wire around the player, his hands shook.

"This is Lieutenant Wyatt Colter. He's a Texas Ranger," said Hardin.

Wide black eyes met Wyatt's gaze. "A Texas Ranger? Seriously?"

Wyatt nodded and allowed himself a tiny smile. "Seriously." He flicked a prong of his badge with his index finger.

"Wow," Kirk breathed.

"Now, Kirk, tell the lieutenant what you told me," Hardin urged.

The boy nodded and licked his lips. "Yesterday I saw a big white pickup driving out toward Daniel's house."

"A big white pickup," Wyatt repeated. He glanced at Hardin, who shook his head once. "What kind of pickup?"

Kirk licked his lips again and looked down at the MP3 player he held. "I don't know. Big."

"Did you see who was driving?" asked Wyatt.

"No, sir."

"Was it Ellie Penateka?" Wyatt quizzed.

Kirk shook his head. "No, sir."

Wyatt looked the boy in the eye. "Are you sure?"

"Yes, sir."

Hardin's chair creaked as he shifted. "Kirk, why'd you come here to tell us this?"

"Daniel asked me and Tim and Andy if we saw anything after we left yesterday." Kirk shrugged. "I told Daniel I saw that pickup, and he said I had to come and tell you."

"Were Tim and Andy with you when you saw it?" Hardin asked.

"No, sir. They left earlier. I stayed to help Daniel put away the tools," replied Kirk.

Wyatt studied the boy. Could he believe him? Taabe hadn't mentioned that one of the boys had stayed longer than the other two. Based on what Wyatt had seen—and what Nina had said—last night, Ellie might well have driven out to Taabe's more than once yesterday.

But Taabe wouldn't have sent Kirk to Sheriff Hardin if the driver of the white pickup had been Ellie.

"Deputy Tolbert drives a white pickup. Was it his?" Wyatt asked, watching Hardin's reaction. The sheriff's jaw flexed.

Kirk shrugged.

"Sheriff, who else drives a big white pickup?" asked Wyatt. He was certain that Kirk knew who the driver was. A glance at the sheriff assured him that he thought the same thing.

"White pickups are pretty common around here. Let's see. Charla Whitley drives one. Reverend Lewis, but his is about twenty years old. And I'm pretty sure one of Jonah Becker's trucks is white." Hardin propped his elbows on his desk. "Kirk, I gotta say it's kind of hard to believe that you saw it but you can't say whose it was."

"The sun was in my eyes, and I didn't think nothing of it. Miss Ellie drives out there all the time," Kirk replied.

"You said it wasn't Ellie," Wyatt reminded him.

"It wasn't," Kirk mumbled.

"How come you're so sure?" Hardin asked. "Didn't you say the sun was in your eyes?"

Kirk frowned and shrugged. "I just know."

"You like Ellie, don't you? Because she's Daniel's friend?"

Kirk nodded. "I guess so. I mean, I like her and all, but it still wasn't her truck."

Hardin stood. "Okay, Kirk, you did the right thing, coming to us. Now I want you to sit in there." He pointed toward a small conference room.

"Are you arresting me?" Kirk gasped.

"No. But I need you to think about that pickup, and why you're so sure it wasn't Ellie," said Hardin.

Kirk shrugged. "I told you, I don't know. It just didn't look like her truck."

Hardin sighed. "What did Daniel say when you told him about the truck?"

Kirk ducked his head.

"Did he *tell* you to say it wasn't Ellie?"

"No, sir. He told me to tell the truth."

"Okay, son. Why don't you draw me a picture of the pickup. I'll let you work on it a few minutes." Hardin gave Kirk a few sheets of paper and a pencil, then let the boy into the conference room and closed the door behind him.

When Hardin came back into his office, Wyatt asked him, "Do you think Taabe told the boy to lie?"

Hardin shook his head. "I've been thinking about that. I don't think so. He wouldn't trust a lie like that to a twelve-year-old. I'm guessing we can eliminate Ellie from the list. As well as the preacher. My guess is Trace Becker. I don't trust him as far as I can throw him. Of course, Charla's a good candidate, too."

"But not Tolbert? You know he told Marcie that if he ever caught her with another man, he'd kill them both."

"Right. So, you going to arrest every guy who's ever said that to his ex-girlfriend?"

"Nope. Just the ones who actually do it." Wyatt sighed. "I guess we've got to search all the white pickups. See if we can pull any mud or other trace evidence that might tell us who planted the hatchet and bone in Daniel's truck."

"And check their alibis," Hardin added. "But right now I'm hungry. I didn't get lunch, and I've got to take a shift out at the site tonight. Kirby and Shane are beat."

"You know, Taabe offered some of his men to help guard the site. I didn't take him up on it, although I was tempted. But what I can do is call on Sentron. They're a security agency we use sometimes. They can send a couple of temporary security guards to help. We've got the resources. They could take one shift."

Wyatt heard a tentative knock.

It was Kirk, holding a sheet of paper. "Uh, Sheriff? I know why it couldn't have been Miss Ellie's truck," he said.

Hardin took the drawing. "Why's that?" he asked.

"'Cause the truck had mud all over the underside, and Miss Ellie's truck ain't ever dirty."

"Good job, son. This is the truck you saw?" asked Hardin.

"Yes, sir. Best I can remember."

The sheriff nodded. "Is that a truck box on the back?"

"Yes, sir. One of those silver ones," Kirk confirmed.

Hardin sighed. "Okay, Kirk. You can go."

"What should I tell my mom? She'll want to know why I'm late."

"Tell her you were helping with an investigation," Hardin replied.

"Yes, sir."

After Kirk left, Wyatt took a look at the drawing. "Tolbert's got a truck box on his truck," he commented.

"So does Charla," Hardin countered.

"And Ellie's?"

"Nope. Not that I recall."

"Well, at least that narrows the number of trucks we have to process. What'd you decide about the security guards?"

"If the Rangers are offering, I'll take 'em. Probably ought to keep the deputies and me on the night shift for now. But maybe the guards could take the early shift so my guys can get some sleep."

"I'll arrange it. They won't be able to start tomorrow, but I might be able to get them for the next morning shift. I'll have the head of the security company call you with their names and credentials."

"Great." Hardin rubbed his eyes. "So where are you headed now?"

Wyatt looked at his watch and grimaced. "I need to get back to the lab. Nina's working over there, and I don't want to take a chance on her being there alone, not even for a few minutes."

Chapter Fifteen

After Nina uploaded the photos of the skull fragments and e-mailed them to the Ranger lab, she set the camera aside and stared at the fragments and the one partially intact skull for a moment.

Her fingers itched to touch them, inspect them, get them under a microscope, but she'd promised herself she'd unload the last box of remains Todd had brought in and get the important pieces into the sink to soak first.

Todd and Julie had wanted to stay and help her examine the skull fragments. In fact they'd begged her, but she'd told them no. They were muddy and exhausted from their days' work. They deserved a night off.

That was one reason she'd sent them away. The other—the most important reason—was that she wanted to be alone when she examined the skull fragments.

In case one of them was Marcie's.

With stoic resolve, she turned her back on the skull bones, pulled on thick work gloves and dug into the box.

Most of the contents were tiny splinters and fragments that had been pulverized by the bulldozer. But there was one large piece in the box. She pulled it out, her pulse skittering.

It was a pelvic bone. Male, unlike the one that sat on the lab table. She brushed at it, but it was caked with dried mud. So she lowered it into the lab sink to let it soak for a few minutes.

Dusting her hands together, she glanced around. It was getting late. The big clock over the front door read six, the time Wyatt had told her he'd be back. A thrill skittered through her.

Wyatt. He'd have the test results they'd been waiting for, but that wasn't the only reason for her quickened heartbeat.

She missed his calm, low voice, the whiff of the mint on his breath, the tingling sensation that filled her whenever he was close to her.

Dear heavens, she was in deeper than she'd realized. Resolutely, she took a deep breath, trying to quell the sense of anticipation.

Reminding herself that it hadn't taken him any time to realize he'd made a mistake in taking her to bed. Otherwise, why would he have rejected her apology so abruptly?

Come on, she berated herself. *Don't fall for the sexy Ranger.*

Deliberately, she turned her attention back to the skull fragments and the partially intact skull. She'd intended to have some information for Wyatt about them. As soon as he got here, he'd be pestering her to stop for the night, and she didn't want to quit until she'd determined whether one of the fragments or the intact skull had belonged to a female.

She'd already tentatively matched the partially intact

skull with the shorter thigh bone, and she couldn't wait to tell Wyatt what she'd found.

Based on the state of the teeth and the skull's age as indicated by the sutures, she was about seventy percent certain it had belonged to Mason Lattimer, the missing antiques broker. On the other hand, no matter whose it was, she was a hundred percent certain he'd been murdered. A couple of matching bone fragments had been splintered by a blow.

The remaining pieces were in two piles, based on their appearance. On casual examination as Todd and Julie were cleaning them, she'd concluded they had belonged to a male, but most of the fragments were small, so she wanted to double-check.

She changed to exam gloves and picked up a piece of skull about two inches in diameter. Its general architecture was rugged, which indicated a male, but there was an odd texture to the surface. It reminded her of the surface of the female pelvic bone from Daniel Taabe's truck.

She fetched the pelvic bone and looked at it and the skull fragment side by side under the lighted magnifying lamp.

Her first impression was right. The two bones had similar markings. Their surfaces appeared to have been etched. Nina frowned and adjusted the light and magnification.

Definitely etched. And not just the outside. The inside, as well. As if with acid. That couldn't have happened in the ground. The soil in this area was alkaline, due to the high limestone content.

She stared at the two pieces. There was another problem, too. The pelvic bone was female. But the skull fragment was definitely male. They matched—and yet they didn't match.

It didn't make sense.

She took close-up photos of them both, hoping the flash would heighten the contrast enough to show the etching in more detail. Then she reached for a scalpel to take scrapings. Using the chemicals here in the lab, she could identify any lingering traces of acid.

She straightened, rubbing the back of her neck. She'd been bent over too long. As soon as she finished with this one test, she would let Wyatt talk her into going back to the inn.

She was looking forward to a long hot bath and…

Her brain flashed on the luxurious pleasure of climbing into a warm, comfortable bed, but in the next nanosecond, her fantasy changed from a bed alone to a bed filled with Wyatt's big, hot, sexy body.

She'd never been completely comfortable waking up next to someone. Even though she'd dated two guys seriously and long enough that she should have.

But this morning had changed everything. Waking up next to Wyatt had felt natural. Right.

Like a really good thing.

And that was a really bad thing.

It looked like they might get the case wrapped up soon. And that meant whatever this *thing* was between Wyatt and her, even though it was brand-new, it had a rapidly approaching expiration date.

That meant she had to rein in her imagination bigtime. No more thinking about how nice it felt to wake up next to him. Or how his slightest touch had awakened her sexuality to a degree she'd never imagined possible.

No. The best thing she could do was to focus all her imagination, all her knowledge, all her energy, on identifying the three sets of remains as quickly as possible.

She carefully scraped the surface of the skull fragment, collected the dust in a beaker and labeled it. Then she did the same with the pelvic bone and a second beaker. As she set the scalpel down, a noise startled her.

A dull metallic thud. She realized she'd heard it before—several times, in fact—since Todd and Julie had left. She squeezed her eyes shut and stretched, trying to loosen up her tense muscles.

She heard the noise again and recognized what it was.

It was the hollow sound of a metal door slamming shut. Probably the door to one of the classrooms or other labs in the building. People leaving for the day.

Wyatt would be here soon. She smiled as she stepped over to the wall shelf that held bottles and jars of common chemicals used in first- and second-year chemistry lab work.

She quickly spotted the substance she needed behind a jar of pure sodium. She carefully lifted the heavy jar and set it on the counter, then stood on tiptoe to reach the bottle labeled Sodium Carbonate. Once she mixed the white powder with the bone dust and added silver nitrate, the resulting reaction would tell her if there was any acid on the bone.

She heard another door slam, and Wyatt's handsome, angular face rose in her vision, setting her pulse to racing. She shook her head. Wyatt was here. *So what? No time to get all girly.*

She dipped a spatula into the sodium carbonate and sprinkled powder over the bone dust. She scanned the bottles on the shelf, looking for silver nitrate solution. Every chemistry lab at every college in the world had a bottle of silver nitrate.

Just as she spotted it, the lights went out.

She jumped, and the spatula hit the granite counter-top with a clatter.

"Wyatt?" she called. But nobody answered.

Her night blindness faded quickly, but the blue-and-purple sunset haze coming through the windows wasn't enough light to see by. Squinting, she scanned the room. Maybe it was a security guard who'd come in and thought the lab was empty.

"Hello?" Her throat spasmed.

The silence was ominous.

Her initial startled response catapulted into outright fear. Someone was in the lab with her.

Someone who wasn't identifying himself.

Stay calm, stay calm. It was probably students playing a prank. Maybe they'd popped in, hit the light switch and run.

Suddenly a flashlight came on, blinding her for an instant. It panned across the room. Nina ducked. Maybe it really was a security guard. She opened her mouth to identify herself. Then dread certainty closed her throat.

No. It wasn't a guard—or a student. Whoever was here with her was not harmless.

Her throat was so tight she couldn't breathe.

Run, her instincts said. *Try to make it to the other door*. But the fire exit was as far away as the front door from where she crouched.

At that instant the flashlight's beam passed over her—and paused.

She froze. Could he see the top of her head?

The harsh beam moved, sweeping the room. Then heavy footsteps echoed on the concrete floor, coming closer. He wasn't even trying to stay quiet. She could hear him breathing, even over the pounding of her heart.

Then an electric hum drowned out all other sounds, and with a dull thump, the emergency lights kicked on.

Adrenaline rushed through her like a cold chill. The lights were dim, but they were better than the pallid glow from the windows.

She stood carefully. The flashlight beam's source was near the door. The beam moved, giving her a view of a large figure clothed all in black. He held the flashlight in his left hand and what looked like a mallet or a large hammer in his right.

Right-handed. Over six feet. One hundred ninety to two hundred pounds. Male. Her brain ticked off the attributes so she could later describe him—assuming she lived.

The flashlight's beam stopped on the bones she'd left on the counter next to the lab sink.

With a satisfied grunt, he rushed toward them.

He was going to destroy her bones.

"No!" she shouted.

The beam pinned her and the man cursed. Brandishing the mallet, he started toward her.

Dear heavens, he hadn't known she was there. She should have stayed quiet. But he was going to destroy her bones.

He hesitated while she stood frozen, pinned like a rabbit under a hawk's piercing gaze. Then he turned and rushed toward the table, with the mallet raised over his head.

Nina knew she couldn't stop him. He was much bigger than she. Even if she had the courage to confront him, she had nothing to use for a weapon.

She watched, helpless, as he swung the mallet.

"No!" The protest was wrung involuntarily from her lips as she cast about for anything she could use to stop him.

But there was nothing, unless…

She reached behind her, feeling for the jar of sodium. Even a freshman lab student knew that pure sodium exploded in water.

Although the jar was heavy, the rock of sodium inside it weighed no more than a couple of ounces. It was suspended in mineral oil to keep it from reacting with moisture in the air. Even if she could toss it into the water-filled sink, it might be too insulated by the mineral oil to flash, much less explode.

Still, it was her only chance to save her evidence. *And her life.*

So she picked up the jar and held it over her head. "Hey!" she shouted. "Over here!" She prayed he'd take the bait and shine the light her way. At least enough so she could take aim at the edge of the sink, where she hoped to smash the jar.

He did.

She threw.

The jar swirled through the air in slow motion, spewing big, glistening drops of mineral oil in spirals.

The intruder ducked.

From somewhere, a voice shouted her name.

The jar hit the edge of the sink and shattered.

She heard a loud splash.

Then with a bright yellow flash, a huge fireball exploded straight up—like a volcano—and bright sparks rained down.

Nina dropped to the floor and covered her head.

DESPERATELY, HIS HEART in his throat, Wyatt slapped the tiled wall with his left hand, searching for a light switch. He clutched his weapon in his right hand, aimed at the blinding explosion. He couldn't see anything but the yellow light, and couldn't hear anything but the bang echoing in his ears.

"Nina!" he shouted, unable to hear even his own voice. *Dear God, don't let her be hurt.*

Then his fingers touched the switches and he flipped them, flooding the lab with light. When his eyes focused, he saw a figure flopping around comically. Each time the intruder tried to get a foothold, he slipped in the thick liquid that coated the floor.

Wyatt squinted, wondering if his eyes were playing tricks, but no, they weren't.

The intruder's hair was smoking.

Holstering his gun, Wyatt crossed the distance between them in two strides and grabbed the man's collar. He dragged him away from the sink, leaving streaks of thick liquid on the concrete floor. He dumped him next to an adjacent lab table and yanked a pair of handcuffs out of his jacket.

Once he'd cuffed the man's hands around the steel table leg, Wyatt straightened and scanned the room. He'd figure out who his perp was later.

Right now he had to find Nina.

The explosion had died as quickly as it had erupted, leaving the room thick with smoke and a distinctly vile and caustic odor, like rotten eggs.

"Nina!" he shouted. "Nina, damn it! Where are you?" He heard something—clothes rustling maybe— and whirled in that direction. "Nina?"

"Wyatt?"

He didn't see her. He wanted to sprint around the counters and tables, searching for her, but while his instincts told him that her voice sounded more relieved than scared, his training kept him from rushing headlong into a trap.

"Are you okay?" he asked, retrieving his gun and holding it at the ready.

She didn't answer. He heard a small sound, like a sob.

His pulse throbbed in his temple. Was there a second intruder? Was he holding Nina? "You've got to answer me, Professor. Tell me what's wrong. Should I call the doctor?"

"No…" Her voice caught. "I'm fine."

He tensed. Her voice sounded stronger, as if she was finally getting it together after a bad scare, but he still wasn't taking any chances. "Can you stand up? I need to see you."

More rustling of clothes. Then he saw the top of her head. He waited until she'd straightened completely and he'd had a good look at her before he lowered his weapon.

Her dark, dark eyes were wide as saucers. Her face looked impossibly pale, and she was shivering, but she was okay.

It took him two tries to slide his gun back into his holster. "Damn it, Professor," he growled. "What were you doing here alone?"

He held out his hand, and with a small cry, Nina ran straight into his arms. For a split second, he pressed his lips against her hair and held her as close as he could, wrapping his arms around her.

She didn't seem to mind. In fact, her arms slid around his waist and held on tight. After only a few seconds, her shivering stopped, and she took a long, shaky breath and sighed, warming the skin of his neck.

"Hey, help me over here!"

It was his perp, complaining.

Nina tensed, then pushed away.

"Help, damn it! My hair's on fire!" yelled the man.

Wyatt squeezed Nina's shoulder, then stalked over and looked down at the man's brown hair. "It's just smoking," he said. He eyed the lab table. Sure enough there was a sink with a sprayer attached to the faucet. "Here, I'll put it out." He jerked the sprayer to the length of its hose and squirted water on the guy's head.

A stream of curses, some in Spanish and some in English, spewed from the guy's mouth. "*Madre de Dios!* What the hell? I'll sue you!"

"Yeah? When? After you're convicted of breaking and entering and assault?" Wyatt barely restrained himself from kicking him in the ribs. He'd attacked Nina.

Luckily for the man, at that moment sirens screamed and blue lights flashed. Within seconds, Sheriff Hardin and three men in fire gear burst through the door.

And stopped in their tracks.

Hardin scowled at Wyatt. "What the…?"

Then two men whose shirts said Security came running in.

"Sheriff, I was just about to call you," Wyatt said. "Looks like this guy was trying to blow up the lab."

"The hell I was," the handcuffed guy said. "That was her!"

Her? Wyatt turned to stare at Nina.

"He was smashing my bones," she said. "I had to stop him."

Hardin cleared his throat. "What's going on here? I need some answers now!"

Wyatt ignored him and the firemen, who headed over to the sink to look at the damage from the explosion. He stepped over to Nina. "Professor? What the hell did you do?"

Nina scraped her teeth across her lower lip, a gesture that in another circumstance would have had him groaning with lust. But all he could do was wait, stunned, to hear how she'd caused the explosion.

"I just threw some sodium into the sink. It's a simple chemical reaction. Sodium oxidizes quickly upon exposure to air and violently when it's dropped into water—"

"Okay," Wyatt said. "I get it. You blew up the sink."

Her eyes widened and she whirled around. "Oh, no!" she cried.

Wyatt sprang toward her and wrapped his arm around her shoulders. "What is it? What's wrong?"

She pointed at the sink. "I destroyed my evidence!"

Chapter Sixteen

Wyatt quickly and efficiently patted down the intruder and found his wallet and car keys in his pants pocket. "Good idea," he muttered. "Carry your ID when you're planning an assault. Saves the law enforcement officers a lot of time. We appreciate it."

He handed the keys over to campus security and ordered them to find and search the car, then take it to Impound.

"Let's go," he said, jerking the perp up and cuffing his hands behind his back. "You're going to have a long night." Looking around, he saw Nina over by the sink, examining the smashed bones. "Nina, come on."

"I can't leave. What about my bones? He smashed one of my skull fragments, and I was in the middle of a test for acid residue."

"Leave it until tomorrow. I'll make sure campus security assigns someone to the lab for tonight."

"They'll be inside? But what if they touch something? I can't afford to have them—"

"Call Todd to spend the night. Can he do some of that testing?"

"Yes, but—"

"Professor, that first night Todd nearly passed out

from excitement just thinking one of the bodies might have been murdered. Let him guard the bones. He'll think he's Indiana Jones. Now come on."

Wyatt hauled his prisoner out of the building and to his Jeep. "Oh, by the way, Jeffrey Marquez," he said, holding the guy's driver's license up. "You have the right to remain silent. Anything you say…"

By the time Wyatt finished reciting Marquez's Miranda rights, they'd reached the Jeep. He shoved him into the backseat and propped a hip against the door to wait for Nina.

Within five minutes, she was walking toward him. Twice she looked back, as if to make sure the lab was locked.

He held up his keys, then tossed them to her.

"What's this?" she asked.

"You drive. I've got to keep an eye on your attacker."

Marquez shifted uncomfortably. Wyatt had the distinct impression that he'd never been in handcuffs before.

Interesting.

When they got to the sheriff's office, Kirby Spears was waiting. He wrangled the prisoner out of the backseat and took him inside.

Nina reached for the door handle.

"No," Wyatt said, laying a hand on her arm. "Take the Jeep. Go back to the inn, and relax. You've had a long day."

Nina's gaze snapped to his, and her dark eyes burned with irritation. "Relax? I'm not going anywhere, cowboy. Not until I find out who this man is and why he tried to destroy my bones."

Wyatt opened his mouth to protest, but he'd seen that look in her eyes before, and he was pretty darn sure she wasn't going to change her mind. So he shrugged, got out and headed inside. Behind him, he heard the driver's-side door slam.

NINA MADE IT INSIDE IN time to hear Wyatt give Deputy Spears an order. "Everything about him. Where he works, lives, hangs out. Where his parents live. Who he's dating. Everything."

When Spears got through writing everything down, he waited, pen poised above paper, but Wyatt didn't say anything else. "Uh, Lieutenant?" Spears said. "What about pulling his record?"

Wyatt nodded. "Right. We need to verify it, but I'll guarantee you, he hasn't got a record."

Nina stepped up beside Wyatt. "You can't know that. He was sneaking around like a pro."

Wyatt leveled his blue gaze at her. "There's no yard-stick or calipers for measuring how an ex-con acts, Professor. It's experience and instinct."

"Okay, then. What in your experience makes you so sure about him?" she asked.

"Today's the first time he's ever had to sit or walk with his hands cuffed behind his back. I'm telling you, he's an amateur," Wyatt insisted. "Whatever he was doing in the lab, either it was to protect himself, or he did it for a friend."

Nina frowned at Wyatt as her brain raced.

"Hey, Professor. What is it?" Wyatt waved his hand in front of her eyes.

"I don't know," she whispered. "Something you said. I don't recognize his name, but I think I've seen him before."

"Where?"

"I can't remember. But I will."

"Lieutenant?" Spears interrupted. "I've got something."

Wyatt stepped around the desk so he could see Kirby's computer monitor. Nina followed him.

"His work ID was in his wallet. He's an emergency medical technician," Spears announced.

"Some EMTs are well versed in anatomy," Nina said.

Wyatt's brows shot up. "Oh, yeah?" He turned on his boot heel and headed into Sheriff Hardin's office.

"Wait," Nina called. But he was already halfway to the door, so she rushed to catch up.

"Hardin, I want to talk to Marquez now," Wyatt declared.

The sheriff didn't even look up. "He's waiting for you in the conference room."

"Okay, then. Thanks," said Wyatt.

Nina suppressed a smile. Wyatt was used to giving orders and taking control. The fact that he and Hardin were practically on equal footing had him off balance. He wasn't used to working alongside someone else. He was more comfortable being in charge of—and responsible for—the people who worked under him.

He stopped with his hand on the doorknob. "Where do you think you're going?"

She almost ran into him. "I want to hear what he has to say." She took a quick breath and continued before Wyatt had a chance to interrupt. "Listen to me, Wyatt. He's an EMT."

"Yeah, you said that."

"This is important. When he broke in, I was about to do a test for acid residue on one of the skull fragments."

Wyatt looked at her for a beat. "Okay, I'll bite. Why?"

"Because the bony surface of the skull was etched. That doesn't happen naturally. That skull was soaked, or at the least washed, in a strong acid. I'm guessing hydrochloric."

"Somebody poured acid on the bones?"

"Not exactly. Acid eats away at a bone's surface. I've seen it before, on skeletons that are used for display. They're cleaned with acid, then bleached before they're put into classrooms. I had to clean one up when I was an undergraduate, for basic anatomy class."

Wyatt's eyes narrowed, then widened. "You think our perp here—"

"He may have planted a skeleton. And was trying to destroy it, or maybe steal it back."

"Why?"

Nina had asked herself that question. The answer fit with what they knew and the clues they'd been given. She met Wyatt's gaze and saw that he'd come to the same conclusion.

She also knew that like her, he couldn't bring himself to state the obvious conclusion—that Marcie was alive and had faked her death.

"Good job, Professor," he said softly as he pushed open the door to the small room and went in.

Nina followed. Jeffrey Marquez was handcuffed by one hand to his chair. He glanced sidelong at them. His face was sullen and he looked tired.

"So what's your story, Jeffrey Marquez?" Wyatt asked.

Marquez didn't respond. He barely acknowledged hearing him. Wyatt glanced at Nina and gave his head an almost imperceptible shake.

She got the message. *Don't talk.*

He sat there, watching Marquez. Every so often, Marquez would give Wyatt a glance, then look back down at the table.

Nina surreptitiously watched the minute hand on her watch. Wyatt stayed quiet and still for a full five minutes. Then he stood abruptly, scraping the wooden chair legs across the hardwood floor with a screech.

Nina jumped, and so did Marquez.

"Okay, then. I've got all I need. We're done here." Wyatt gestured to Nina. "I think we'll go with breaking and entering, destruction of state property in furtherance of a crime, interfering with an ongoing investigation and, of course—" he turned the doorknob and opened the door "—attempted murder."

As Nina walked past Wyatt and through the door, she heard him whisper, "Wait for it. One…two… three…"

"Hold it!" Marquez yelled, his face draining of color. "Wait a minute. Nobody said anything about attempted murder."

Wyatt turned casually. "While I was in here, nobody said anything, period."

"If anybody's guilty of attempted murder, it's her," Marquez accused. "She set off a huge explosion right next to me. Nearly blew me up!"

Wyatt turned back toward the door.

"No, wait." Marquez tried to stand, but with his wrist handcuffed to the chair arm, he couldn't. "I swear, I don't know anything about any murder!"

"I didn't say murder," Wyatt replied. "I said *attempted* murder. But first things first. What were you doing in the lab?"

"I was just looking for something that belonged to me. I was hoping to get it and get out before anyone saw me."

"Something? What?"

Marquez shook his head and laughed uneasily. "I can

promise you, it has nothing to do with the bodies you're looking for."

Wyatt leaned over the table. "Listen to me, Marquez. If you were dancing any faster around my questions, you'd screw your head right off your shoulders. Now, I'll be happy to help you with that, but I'd like to get a straight answer first." He sat down. "Now, does your breaking and entering and destruction of evidence have anything to do with the fact that you're an EMT, and one of our skeletons has been washed in acid?"

Marquez jerked in surprise. "How'd you…? I mean, what makes you say that?"

"Not me. Dr. Jacobson." Wyatt jerked his thumb in Nina's direction. "She's a forensic anthropologist. So she notices things like acid-etched skeletons."

Marquez turned to her. "Then you know that skeleton has nothing to do with your case."

But Wyatt didn't give Nina a chance to answer. He broke in. "Nothing to do with my case? It was right there in the middle of my crime scene, with the other bones."

The young man hesitated as sweat broke out on his forehead. After a few seconds, he shrugged. "Okay, look. The bones came from the medical school. They supplied skeletons to area schools. I'd sneak into the room where the students would clean the bones, and grab something whenever I had the chance." He grinned nervously. "For a prank. That's all."

Nina gasped, and her fingers flew to her mouth.

Both Wyatt and Marquez turned to stare at her.

"I know where I've seen you before," she said, her voice muffled by her fingers. "You dated Marcie."

"Lady, I've never met you. I don't know what you're talking about," Marquez replied.

She turned to Wyatt. "I recognize that grin. She e-mailed me a photo of the two of them. They were friends who dated off and on." Her heart was pounding, but her brain was racing even faster.

EMT. Marcie. Terrified.

"You kidnapped Marcie," Nina cried. "You pulled her hair out by the roots and stuck the necklace in it and planted it at the burial site with the remains, didn't you? Making sure we'd be able to find it."

Marquez looked panicked. He spread his hands. "I swear, I don't—"

Wyatt stood. "You're wasting my time here. If you don't start talking in the next fifteen seconds, I'm charging you with everything I listed, plus resisting arrest, plus anything else I can get away with. In fact, I *will* add murder. The murder of Marcie James."

Marquez's face turned a sickly pale. "No! No! You can't. Please. Marcie's not dead!"

Wyatt glanced at Nina. She was frozen in shock, her eyes wild and bright as she stared at Marquez.

"How do you know that? What did you have to do with Marcie James's kidnapping?" Wyatt quizzed.

"I was… I just did what Marcie wanted me to do," Marquez explained. "You don't get it. She planned the fake kidnapping. She wanted to escape. Needed to. She was sure somebody was trying to kill her."

Nina's heart nearly stopped. Marcie had faked her own kidnapping. She'd disappeared on purpose. She'd almost killed Wyatt.

Everything Nina had believed for the past two years was suddenly turned upside down. She'd blamed Wyatt for causing her best friend's death. But now she had to face the truth.

Her best friend had almost killed the man Nina loved.

Loved?

Dear heavens, did she love him? Her heart was beating again, so fast and so loudly she was sure Wyatt and Marquez could hear it. It wasn't possible. Not after three days.

Why couldn't she take a hint? His brusque dismissal of her apology this morning should have squelched any blossoming attraction caused by their night of lovemaking. But strangely, it hadn't.

One night, and she was already in too deep. Not only had the sex been the best she'd ever had, but lying next to him, protected by his strong body, had awakened feelings inside her that she'd long feared she would never experience again.

She'd spent her childhood surrounded by a shield of protection. Her father and her older brother had taken care of her. They'd been her knights in shining armor. But then her dad had died, and less than a year later, her older brother was gone, too, killed overseas in combat.

The feeling that nothing could harm her had died with them.

Until now.

Dear heavens, what was she going to do when this investigation was over? Now that Wyatt had made her love him?

His voice interrupted her thoughts. "Did Marcie's plans include trying to kill a Texas Ranger?" he thundered, his expression dark and ominous.

Marquez winced. "Hey, Marcie gave me that gun. I'd never shot a gun before in my life. Didn't you see how wild the shots were? It was a complete accident that I hit you. I'm sorry, man."

"You're sorry?" Nina burst out. To her surprise,

Wyatt leaned back in his chair and appeared to relax. It was a few seconds before he spoke.

"Where is she?" he muttered.

Marquez's eyes widened.

"Damn it!" Wyatt's fist came down on the table, bouncing the pens. "Where. Is. She?"

Marquez shrugged. "I—I don't know, man. She hid out with me for a few days. Then she said she had to disappear. Said she had a friend who would help her."

"Who?" asked Wyatt.

Marquez shrugged again. "I don't know—"

"Don't give me that. Male or female? Here in town?" Wyatt quizzed.

"I said I don't know."

Wyatt glared at him. "Listen, bud. Right now you are on the hook for a very serious crime that carries serious time. The only way I can help you is if you cooperate. So if you know anything about why Marcie felt she had to disappear, you'd better start talking."

"All I know is she was afraid of somebody. Terrified. And she wouldn't tell me who."

"You're going to have to do better than that."

"I swear, man. She said if I knew, I'd be in danger, too."

"So you lied, stole and nearly killed for her, and you didn't know why you were doing it?"

Marquez wiped the sweat off his face with his shirt-sleeve and then eyed Wyatt narrowly. "Just exactly what can you do for me? I mean, if I tell you who I *think* she might have been afraid of?"

Nina watched Wyatt's expression turn black and his fists clench. She held her breath, but to his credit, he didn't go across the table at Marquez.

"I'll consider recommending assault with intent, rather than attempted first-degree murder," Wyatt said.

Marquez swallowed visibly. "I think she was scared of her ex."

Wyatt's expression didn't change.

"I knew it!" Nina burst out. "I knew it! Marcie was afraid Shane would kill her."

Chapter Seventeen

It took another hour or so for Wyatt to wrap up the paperwork and call a Ranger from Austin to come and take Marquez into custody, but finally, by eleven, Wyatt and Nina were back at the Bluebonnet Inn. As they climbed the stairs, Wyatt saw how tired she was by the droop of her shoulders and the heaviness of her step.

At the top of the stairs, he put his hand on the small of her back and guided her toward her door. "You're exhausted. Get some sleep," he said gently. "I won't wake you up until the last possible moment tomorrow."

She started to shake her head.

"No arguments. You'll need it, trust me. We've still got a lot of work ahead."

"Wyatt—"

He bent and stole a quick kiss. "I won't let you miss any of the good stuff."

"Promise?"

"Promise. Now give me your key."

She sent him an odd look, but handed it over.

He opened her door for her, instructed her to sleep for at least eight hours, then unlocked his own door and went inside.

He knew exactly what the look she'd shot at him

meant. She didn't understand why he was acting as though nothing had happened between them.

He couldn't blame her. He didn't understand himself. All he knew was that until this case was over, he couldn't afford to let his guard down again. His strengths were his focus and determination. He had to pour all his energy and concentration into the job at hand. Saving the innocent and catching the guilty was his purpose. For him, anything that took his mind off the job had to be ignored. Anything like sexual attraction or falling in love.

As he showered, he tried to figure out why pouring every ounce of his energy into seeking justice wasn't satisfying. Not this time. For the first time in his life, he was having trouble compartmentalizing the separate parts of his life.

He dried off, pulled on sweatpants and lay down with a sigh. He was so tired, his body ached. But when he turned over, his nose picked up on the subtle scent of roses.

With a growl, he turned over the other way, trying to ignore the longing that filled his heart, the longing to have Nina lying next to him. Her soft, even breaths were more soothing and relaxing than anything he'd ever experienced.

How was he going to sleep without her next to him?

BY NINE O'CLOCK the next morning Wyatt and Nina were back at the sheriff's office. Nina wanted to read Marquez's statement, to see just exactly what he'd said about Marcie.

Wyatt hadn't heard back about the examination of the boot casts, so that was his first question for Hardin.

"Yeah," the sheriff said. "I've got the results right

here. Turns out the footprints from the crime scene are Shane's. The indentations on the heels were made by taps. Shane wears rubber taps on the heels of his boots."

"Damn it. Obviously his prints would be there. All the prints couldn't have been his, could they? Didn't your deputy take more than one casting?"

"He took seven. Three were too smeared to identify. The other four were consistent with Shane's boots."

"So we still don't know anything about who attacked him." A faint memory came to Wyatt. "You know what? I need to talk to the doctor. I've got Nina's photos of Tolbert's head wound. There was a faint redness in a similar shape next to the wound. Like a hesitation wound."

"Hesitation wound? What are you saying? That Shane hit *himself* over the head?"

Wyatt shrugged. "It's within the realm of possibility. That's why I want to show the pictures to the doctor. Get his opinion."

Hardin shook his head. "Fine. I can't stop you. But I'm telling you, I find it hard to believe that Shane would risk his job. He's worked really hard to get where he is."

"I've got to cover all the bases…" Wyatt was interrupted by the ringing of his cell phone. "This is Lieutenant Colter." He heard nothing but rapid, shaky breathing on the other end of the phone. "Hello? Who is this?"

"I need help! Daniel's been shot. At his house. Please hurry." The feminine voice was a whisper, but the words might as well have been a scream.

"Who is this?" Wyatt demanded, shooting up out of his chair. His hand rested briefly on the hilt of his weapon as he caught Hardin's eye. "Ellie?"

Classified Cowboy

The sheriff got the message. He stood and grabbed his holster.

To Wyatt's right, Nina bounded up.

"Talk to me. Tell me where you are." Wyatt listened, but all he heard was the woman's quick, shallow breaths.

"Just hurry, or he's going to die," the woman gasped.

The phone went dead.

"Damn it," Wyatt spat.

Hardin was already headed out the door, with Nina right on his heels. "What's going on?" he threw back over his shoulder. "Who was that?"

"A woman. Said Daniel Taabe had been shot. At his house," Wyatt called.

Outside, Hardin headed for his truck, and Wyatt sprinted toward his Jeep.

Nina climbed in beside him.

As they pulled away, Mayor Sadler and Jerry Collier walked out of the courthouse. The mayor raised his hand to wave, then frowned. Collier looked shocked, and Wyatt could see his prominent Adam's apple bob from where he sat.

Wyatt checked the last call that came in and dialed the number. He listened to the rings until voice mail picked up. Sure enough, the voice was Taabe's. Wyatt cut the connection. "That call came from Daniel Taabe's house," Wyatt said as he followed Hardin's truck onto the road to Taabe's house.

"Did you give Ellie your cell number?" Nina asked Wyatt.

Wyatt muttered a curse. "I gave out my card to everybody I talked to. So yeah. She has it. Charla Whitley has it. And of course, I gave Daniel a card, too, so anyone at his house could find my number. The call could have come from just about anybody."

It took them less than five minutes to get to Taabe's

house. Wyatt pulled up beside Hardin's truck. "Stay here until we clear the house," he ordered Nina as he jumped out of the Jeep and hit the ground running, drawing his weapon.

The house looked dark, and the driveway was empty. He glanced around, wondering if Taabe had put his truck in the barn or behind the house. He slowed down and crept up to the front door, a few steps behind Hardin.

Hardin pounded on the front door. "Daniel Taabe. Police! Open up!"

Nothing.

"Police!" Hardin yelled again. "We're coming in!" He glanced back at Wyatt, who nodded, then kicked the door in.

Inside, a hallway separated the living area from the bedrooms. Wyatt took the right side, and Hardin the left.

Wyatt checked the living room, including the coat closet.

"Front bedroom clear," he heard Hardin say.

"Living room clear," he answered. He sidled along the wall to the door that led into a small dining room. He could see the kitchen beyond it.

"Second bedroom clear," called Hardin.

The tiny dining room couldn't have hidden a mouse. Wyatt stepped through it and into the kitchen. As soon as he rounded the door, he saw the blood and Daniel Taabe's black hair.

"Back bedroom clear."

"Hardin! In here!"

The sheriff appeared through a door on the left side of the kitchen. "Damn it," he said when he saw Taabe's body.

Wyatt leaned over and pressed his fingers against Taabe's carotid artery, although he knew it was futile. "He's dead. I'm going to get the professor."

He ran through the front of the house and outside and waved at Nina. To his relief, she waved back and then got out of the Jeep carrying her kit.

"I can tell by your face," she said when she reached his side. "Daniel's dead, isn't he?"

Wyatt nodded, wondering when he'd become so easy to read.

"How?"

"We haven't examined him yet."

When they got to the kitchen, Hardin was crouching beside Taabe's body. He spoke without looking up. "He hasn't been dead long. Blood hasn't had time to coagulate."

Nina snapped on a glove and knelt beside Taabe. She touched the edge of the pool of blood. "There's not even a demarcation line. What do you think, Reed? An hour?"

"Or less," said the sheriff.

"COD?" she asked.

"The cause of death is a gunshot wound to the upper chest," Hardin observed. "Through and through, judging by the amount of blood on the floor. Probably at close range."

"Through and through," Wyatt said. "Then we have a bullet."

Hardin nodded. "I haven't turned him over yet. Have you got your camera? I'll get started photographing the scene."

Nina took her camera out of her kit and handed it to Hardin. "Go ahead." She stood. "What do you think? Did he confront the person who planted the bone and hatchet in his truck?"

Wyatt shook his head. "I wish I knew. First thing I want to do is question Ellie Penateka. She may have been the last person to see him alive."

Nina looked at him questioningly.

"There, on the kitchen counter." Wyatt gestured with his head. "Two coffee cups. One with lipstick on the brim."

Nina looked where Wyatt had gestured. Sure enough, there were two large yellow coffee cups sitting on the counter, along with two crumpled paper napkins. She took in the rest of the kitchen. There were dishes that matched the cups on the drain board. She walked over to the sink. On the shelf above lay a woman's turquoise ring.

She was about to point it out to Wyatt when her phone rang. She glanced at the display. She didn't recognize the number. "Hello?"

"N-Nina? Oh, thank goodness I got you. I think my phone's about to go dead."

Nina almost dropped the phone. She knew that voice. It was a voice she had known for ten years but hadn't heard in more than two. A voice she'd thought she would never hear again. "Marcie?"

"Yes..." Marcie's voice broke.

"Dear heavens, Marcie. Where are you? What's going on?"

Wyatt, still crouched next to Daniel's body, twisted and sent her a shocked glance. She met his gaze, knowing her own expression was as stunned as his.

Marcie was talking to her on her phone.

Marcie was *alive*.

"You're there, aren't you? At Daniel's. He's dead, isn't he?" Marcie sobbed.

"I'm sorry, Marcie. Yes." It was hard to talk. Her lips felt numb. Her throat was constricted. "Where are you? What were you thinking?"

"Listen to me, Nina. I don't have time to explain. I'm at the cabin—the one above Dead Man's Road."

"Dead Man's Road?"

"It's the road out to the crime scene. The cabin is on the ridge above. Daniel told me to come here—"

"Daniel told you? Marcie, were you here? Did you see who shot Daniel?"

"I was…in the basement, taking a nap. I heard the shot, and then I heard a vehicle start up. When I came upstairs, Daniel was on the floor." Marcie took a shaky breath. "I swear, Nina, I wanted to call a doctor, but Daniel told me to take his truck and get to safety. I didn't want to leave him."

"Marcie, tell me what…" Nina suddenly found herself empty-handed. Wyatt had grabbed her phone.

"Marcie," he snapped. "It's Wyatt Colter. Where are you?" He listened for a second, then turned his head toward the sheriff, who had pulled out his cell phone and was about to dial. He shook his head violently and held up a hand. "Don't call anybody. Who's at the crime scene this morning?"

"Shane," Hardin replied.

Wyatt cursed. "Marcie, can you see the crime scene or the road? No? Well, Shane is on duty over there. You want us to call him?"

Nina heard Marcie's terrified voice through the phone. "No! Please. Not Shane."

"Okay, okay. I understand. We won't. You stay put. I'm on my way." Wyatt hung up and handed the phone back to Nina. "Damn it."

Hardin spoke up. "I'll get Kirby to head over there—"

"No. I'm going. Marcie knows I'm coming. Just be ready, in case I need backup." Wyatt already had his keys in his hand and was headed for the door.

Nina followed him.

At the door, he turned, pinning her with those intense blue eyes. "What the hell are you doing?"

She stood up to him, refusing to be intimidated by his expression or his attitude. "Marcie was dead. Now she's alive," she said. "I have to see her."

"There's no way I'm taking you into such a potentially dangerous situation," Wyatt replied.

She lifted her chin and gave him back stare for stare. "I will steal a car if I have to," she said. "But I *will* see my friend. The only way you're going to stop me is by arresting me or knocking me out."

His eyes glinted dangerously, and for a small space of time, she almost believed he might accept her challenge. But in the next split second his gaze wavered, and she knew she'd won.

She didn't have time to even sigh with relief, because Wyatt was out the door and loping to his Jeep. She barely made it into the passenger seat by the time he had the engine running and in reverse.

Neither one of them said anything on the way. Wyatt's Jeep ate up the roads, kicking up clouds of white dust. It hadn't rained since that first night.

Nina's seat belt strained against her midsection as Wyatt careered onto Dead Man's Road and immediately took an abrupt turn up a steep back road.

Several bumpy, dusty moments later, Nina saw a weathered cabin through a stand of trees.

Wyatt stopped the car. "Stay here."

"Fat chance, cowboy." Nina's heart was pounding in anticipation of seeing her friend. Marcie had lied, she'd broken the law, she'd pretended to be dead, but Nina still loved her.

Marcie was her friend.

Wyatt grunted but didn't say anything else until they were out of the Jeep and headed toward the front door. "You think you can stay by my side?"

"It would be my pleasure," she murmured.

Wyatt sent her an intense sidelong glance. An odd expression lit his face, but as soon as it had appeared, it was gone, and he was back to being the tough, brave Texas Ranger. He drew his weapon. "We'll go in on this side of the cabin. There's only one window, so there's less likelihood that they'll spot us."

"It's just Marcie. Why…?"

His hand went up, palm out. "Follow my orders or go back to the car."

Nina bit her lip. "Yes, sir."

"When I move, you move. *Not before*. If I do this—" he held up his fist at shoulder height "—you stop, and don't move until I wave you forward. Got it?"

"Got it."

Nina's answer was drowned out by the crack of a gunshot, which shattered the silent air around them. She heard a thud to her right. A puff of dust or smoke rose from the trunk of a tree not three feet away.

Before she could react, two more shots split the air. One of them came close enough that her heart jolted hard in her chest—so hard it could have been a blow.

Wyatt's hand wrapped around her wrist and pulled her down beside him. She hadn't even noticed him crouch down.

"That was close," she whispered, putting her hand over her heart. "I nearly jumped out of my…" She drew back her hand and looked at it. The fingertips were coated with red paint.

Then her eyes lost focus and she felt dizzy and faint.

What if it wasn't paint? she thought.

What if it was *blood?*

"Wyatt?" she whispered.

Chapter Eighteen

Wyatt looked in horror at Nina's stained fingers, then at her shirt, where dark red blood was spreading.

She'd been shot.

"Nina!" He shoved his gun into his shoulder holster and dove toward her. He ripped her shirt apart, popping the buttons.

Blood coated the area between her shoulder and neck, and dripped down around her left breast.

"Oh, God, Nina!" He took a piece of her shirt and used it to wipe away as much blood as he could. "I knew it," he groaned. "I knew something would happen to you."

He'd gotten her shot. The thing he'd most feared had come true. He'd sworn to protect her, and he'd failed.

He peered at the wound. It was her shoulder, in that sweet spot between the shoulder joint and the clavicle. Thank God, it hadn't pierced any organs or broken any bones. He folded the cloth and pressed it against the entry wound.

Mere inches above his head, a bullet whizzed by. And another. Whoever had shot Nina hadn't stopped. He was still shooting. Still aiming to kill.

"Hey, Professor," Wyatt muttered. "You're going to be fine. All I need to do is lift you up a little bit so I can see your back. It might hurt, but I promise you you're going to be okay."

"I trust you," she whispered.

His arms shook as he slid them around her back and lifted, giving her as much support as he could. He didn't feel any wetness. A good sign? Or a bad one?

She moaned as he shifted her slightly so he could see her back. No exit wound. That meant the bullet was still in there. He ran his palm along her skin.

There. The small lump he felt had to be the bullet. He needed to get her to a hospital now and get that bullet taken out.

But he couldn't. His priority, once he'd assured himself that Nina wasn't in mortal danger, was to stop the gunman and save Marcie.

This time.

Another shot rang out, too close. Wyatt ducked and covered Nina with his body. "Don't worry. I've got you," he whispered.

"I know." He heard the strain in her voice. She was in pain. A lot of pain, and there was nothing he could do about it.

"Listen to me," he whispered in her ear. "I need you to stay here. Stay hidden. Can you call Hardin for backup? Because whoever shot you is in there. And I've got to stop him."

Nina nodded. Her lips were pressed together and white at the edges. Her eyes were closed. But she held out her hand for the phone. "I'll call him. You save Marcie," she mumbled.

Wyatt pressed his lips to her forehead. "I'm going to save both of you."

"I know." When he gave her the phone, she grabbed his hand and squeezed it. "Wyatt, be careful."

Wyatt squeezed back. Then he moved carefully, staying low, until he was twenty feet away from Nina. He didn't want the shooter in the cabin to have any idea where she was. He needed to draw the fire away from her.

And he needed to get inside that cabin.

He raised himself up enough to aim and shoot at the open side window of the cabin. Then he ducked. The shooter responded with three quick rounds.

Wyatt stayed low, sneaking from one scrubby tangle of sagebrush to another. He fired at the window once, twice, three times. Then he took several shots at the front porch. He knew that, although the bang would sound in the same place, the bullets would hit or ricochet off the wood on the front corner of the cabin. The shooter's perception of where the sounds came from would be confused, unless he was very experienced.

Sure enough, the shots from inside the house stopped.

Wyatt used the lull to duck and roll, ending up next to the rear corner of the cabin. He pushed himself to his feet, his back against the rough plank wall. Then he sidled toward the back and peered around the corner.

Sure enough there was a rear door. Beyond it he saw the nose of a white pickup.

Damn. The shallow print of boots in the dust led from the pickup to the wooden stoop. Someone had used this door recently. Someone who'd driven a white pickup.

Wyatt crept over to the door and gingerly turned the knob. It turned easily and quietly. A little surprising for such a dilapidated cabin.

He could hear shots coming from the front of the

cabin. His stomach clenched. Nina wouldn't have stood up, would she? Not after he'd told her to stay down.

Surely not. Still, she was stubborn and bullheaded. Just about as bullheaded as he was. But she was wounded, damn it.

He suppressed the urge to yell out a warning to her. If he did that, he'd be handing the shooter a lot of valuable information on a silver platter. Where he was, and that there were two of them at least.

Not knowing what to expect, he pushed open the door and angled around it, leading with his weapon. He found himself in a mudroom, which led to the large main room. The interior of the cabin was bathed in shadow, the only light coming from two bare windows.

On one side of Wyatt was a short hallway. He started that way but stopped when he heard a muffled curse and the unmistakable sound of a magazine being ejected from a semiautomatic handgun.

The shooter was out of bullets. He stiffened and laid his back against the wall, preparing to round the corner with his weapon ready to shoot. Before he could make his move, he heard a magazine being slapped into place. The man had reloaded.

More shots rang out.

At least the guy didn't know Wyatt was behind him. After all, it hadn't been more than two minutes since he'd left Nina, and it was an understatement to say that he'd been sparing with his shots.

But if another minute passed without a response from outside, the shooter would suspect that something was up. So Wyatt had to move fast.

Fast and smart.

He decided to take a chance and peek around the door into the main room, to get an idea of where the shooter was. From the sounds, he figured the man had moved from the side window to the front, which meant his back should be to Wyatt.

Carefully and quickly, he took off his hat and peered around the corner. What he saw shocked and sickened him.

Sprawled on the floor near the fireplace was the body of a young woman with blond hair. Wyatt didn't need a long look to know the woman was Marcie James.

Or to know that she was dead. Her sightless eyes caught the light from the windows.

Standing beyond her, at the open front window, was Shane Tolbert, straining to peek through the heavy curtains, his weapon aimed at something Wyatt couldn't see.

At that instant, Wyatt's ears picked up the faint sound of a car engine. Without wasting precious time assessing whether Tolbert had heard it, he acted.

"Tolbert, don't move." He kept his voice low and steady.

Tolbert tensed, then started to turn.

"I said don't move."

"Lieutenant Colter?" The deputy raised his hands slowly and let his gun dangle from his index finger.

"Drop the gun."

"Thank God it's you," Tolbert said, lowering his arms.

"Slowly!"

Tolbert set the gun on the floor and straightened. His face was pale. His eyes were wide, and a trickle of blood ran down his neck.

"Did you catch whoever was shooting at me? I thought I was dead, too." His gaze dropped to Marcie's body, and he shook his head, as if he couldn't believe his eyes.

Wyatt frowned. Tolbert was acting like Wyatt had rescued him. Like they were on the same side. But Wyatt didn't have time to waste on questions. Nina was out there, wounded, hurting, possibly bleeding to death.

The vehicle's engine got louder, and Wyatt heard the crunch of tires on limestone rocks.

"Put your hands behind your back and turn around," Wyatt ordered.

"What? You think I did it? Are you nuts?"

Wyatt gestured with his gun barrel. "Don't push me, Tolbert. Do it! And spread your legs."

The deputy obeyed. "I understand how this looks. Believe me. But you've got to listen to me. Marcie called me. She wanted to meet me up here. I couldn't believe it was her—after all this time."

Wyatt snapped the cuffs shut around the deputy's wrists just as a second vehicle roared to a stop outside.

God, let it be the ambulance.

"Colter, you've got to believe me. Somebody hit me over the head as soon as I walked in the door. When I woke up, I saw Marcie lying there…" Tolbert's voice broke.

The door burst open, and Reed Hardin stepped in, brandishing his weapon.

"Sheriff! Tell him I loved Marcie," Tolbert yelled.

Hardin's surprised gaze took in the scene before him. "What the hell?"

"Why were you shooting at us?" Wyatt prodded.

Tolbert drew in a shaky breath. "I thought whoever killed Marcie was trying to kill me."

Wyatt had to hand it to the deputy. He was convincing. But was he innocent? "Save it, Tolbert. I'm taking you in for the murder of Marcie James. Shane Tolbert, you have the right to remain silent—"

The sound of an engine interrupted Wyatt. Red blinking lights glanced off the walls.

"Hardin, you got this?" Wyatt asked. "Because Nina's out there. Tolbert shot her."

"Sure. Go." The sheriff sounded slightly dazed.

"I shot Nina? Oh, no!" Tolbert moaned.

Wyatt shoved his gun into its holster as he rushed out the door. But he was too late. The ambulance, carrying its precious cargo, disappeared into a cloud of white dust down the steep back road.

WYATT RUSHED IN THROUGH the emergency room's automatic doors and headed straight toward the desk. "Nina Jacobson. Gunshot wound," he snapped.

The woman behind the desk recoiled. "What? Who?"

From the corner of his eye, Wyatt saw a hospital security guard start toward him.

"Lieutenant Colter, Texas Ranger. I need to check on Nina Jacobson."

The woman looked at his badge, the guard and then the computer screen in front of her. "Uh, cubicle eight," she said, pointing to Wyatt's left. "That way."

Wyatt took off, nearly running into a steel cart. He skirted the edge of the cart and skidded to a stop in front of the cubicle labeled eight. When he shoved the curtain aside, his heart skipped a beat.

Nina was lying on a hospital bed, seemingly surrounded by tubes and wires. Her face was impossibly pale against her ink-black hair. An oxygen tube was anchored to her nostrils, and the electronic display on the box beside her bed beeped in rhythm with her heartbeat.

A nurse finished injecting a yellow liquid into a port on the IV tubing that led from a huge bandage above her wrist to the bag of fluid hanging beside the bed. The nurse, whose multicolored jacket had puppies and kittens cavorting on it, frowned at him.

"I'm Lieutenant Wyatt Colter, Texas Ranger," he said defensively. "She's my…my—"

His throat tightened. His what? His colleague? His Professor? His *love?*

Nina opened her eyes and sent him a ghost of a smile. "Hey, cowboy. Still as eloquent as ever, I see."

"You forgot charming," he replied.

"No," she muttered. "I didn't forget." She licked her lips and lifted her left hand to adjust the oxygen tube.

He caught her hand in his. "Can she have some water?"

The nurse glowered at him. "No. She's about to go into surgery."

"Surgery?" Adrenaline sent Wyatt's heart pounding. He knew the bullet in her shoulder had to come out. But knowing it in his head and seeing her—pale and weak and being prepped to go under the knife were two very different things.

"I'll be right back, Ms. Jacobson." The nurse left the cubicle, yanking the curtain closed behind her.

Wyatt couldn't take his eyes off Nina.

She squeezed his hand. "Don't look at me like that," she said hoarsely.

He grimaced. The oxygen was already making her throat raw. "Like what?"

"Like I'm about to—"

He stopped her words with his fingers. "Don't even joke about that," he said gruffly.

"What happened?" she croaked.

"You don't need to worry about that right now."

"Wyatt, I need to know who was shooting at us. It was Shane, wasn't it?"

He nodded.

"Did he kill Daniel?"

"I don't know."

She coughed.

"Now, hush. You need to rest and stay calm." He bent forward and kissed her. Her lips were dry, so he ran his tongue along them to moisten them.

She laughed softly. "Thank you," she whispered. Then she kissed him back.

His heart leapt and stuck in his throat. The feel of her lips had sent signals that his body didn't want to ignore. Signals that were bound to cause him a lot of embarrassment when that nurse came back.

But far stronger than his physical need was the fierce protective urge that filled him.

"I was supposed to keep you safe," he said, pressing his forehead against hers. "And I didn't."

She stiffened. "Oh, Wyatt..."

He knew the leap her brain had made, because his had made the same instantaneous jump. She was thinking about Marcie.

God, he'd failed to protect her friend—twice.

"Wyatt, tell me about Marcie."

He pulled back and reluctantly met her gaze. But for the life of him, he couldn't think of the right words.

Or any words.

She touched his cheek with her left hand. "It's okay. I know she didn't make it. I heard the radio in the ambulance when Reed called for the ME. She was pronounced dead on the scene. Did Shane shoot her?"

He nodded. "He claims he found her like that, and somebody hit him on the head. I don't believe him. He had the gun in his hand."

"Could you tell anything about the blood spatter? Or the angle of entry?"

He couldn't help but smile. "No, Professor. I didn't have much time for that. I arrested him on the spot, though, and turned him over to Sheriff Hardin. I've already called Ranger Sergeant Olivia Hutton, my crime scene analyst. I've made sure she understands to check everything thoroughly—herself."

"Good." Nina's voice was hoarse and her eyes were filled with tears. "Poor Marcie."

Wyatt sat on the edge of the bed and laid his palm against her cheek. "God, Nina. I'm so sorry." He muttered as his heart wrenched in grief and regret. "I was too late—again."

Nina's fingers brushed his lips. "No," she said vehemently. "No you weren't. You did everything you could. Today and two years ago. It took me a while to realize what kind of man you are. It shouldn't have taken that long. I should have known the first time I met you."

Wyatt caught her hand in his and squeezed it. He couldn't look at her.

She went on. "I should have known that badge was more than just a piece of silver that gives you the authority to bring in the bad guys. That piece of silver represents you, down to your soul."

"Nina, I—"

"Shh. Marcie got Marcie killed. And I'm afraid she got Daniel killed, too. If she'd been truthful with you—if she had accepted your protection—then she might be alive today." She shook her head. "I lost my friend two years ago."

Wyatt's heart was still pounding, but now not with fear or lust. "God, I love you."

Nina blinked. She knew she was hazy from the drugs they'd given her, but was she hallucinating, too? Did she imagine him saying what she wanted so badly to hear? "What did you say?"

Wyatt's face had gone pale, which wasn't a good sign. "I said I love you—I think."

Those last two words wrenched the breath right out of her. It took her two tries to be able to speak. "You— you think?"

He shook his head and mumbled a curse. "No, I don't…I mean, I didn't…"

She bit her lips to keep from moaning aloud. She lay back against the pillows. "It's okay, cowboy."

He growled deep in his throat. "Look, none of this is coming out the way I wanted it to." He took a deep breath. "I love you. I want to marry you, damn it!"

A clatter of metal against metal announced the nurse's return. She stopped, an amused look on her face. "Wow! How romantic," she drawled. "Now if you're done with that lovely proposal, the bride needs to go to surgery."

To Nina's drowsy amusement, Wyatt's face turned red. He jumped up from his seat on the bed. "Right. Sure," he stammered. "I'll, uh—"

The nurse held up a syringe. "They're on their way from the operating room to get you now. After this shot, you'll be pretty sleepy. So if you've got anything to say, you'd better say it now."

Nina smiled at her flustered Texas Ranger. "My charming, eloquent hero. It's settled, then. I want to marry you, too, damn it."

"You do?" Wyatt's face was still red as a beet.

The nurse snorted as she injected the drug. "How could she pass up such a sweet proposal? You'd better kiss her fast. She's about to nod off to sleep."

Nina lifted her head for his kiss, which was the

sweetest, most tender kiss she'd ever experienced. "Are you running off to chase bad guys?" she murmured.

"Sheriff Hardin and Sergeant Hutton can handle the bad guys for now. I'm not going anywhere until you're all sewn up. I'll be right here when you wake up. You can count on it."

She could no longer keep her eyes open, but she knew that Wyatt Colter, Texas Ranger, was a man of his word. "I know," she whispered, smiling.

* * * * *

The Silver Star of Texas: Comanche Creek
continues next month with SHOTGUN SHERIFF
by Dolores Fossen. Look for it wherever
Harlequin Intrigue books are sold!

Fan favorite Leslie Kelly is bringing her readers a
fantasy so scandalous,
we're calling it FORBIDDEN!

Look for
PLAY WITH ME
Available February 2010
from Harlequin® Blaze™.

"AREN'T YOU GOING TO SAY 'Fly me' or at least 'Welcome Aboard?'"

Amanda Bauer didn't. The softly muttered word that actually came out of her mouth was a lot less welcoming. And had fewer letters. Four, to be exact.

The man shook his head and tsked. "Not exactly the friendly skies. Haven't caught the spirit yet this morning?

"Make one more airline-slogan crack and you'll be walking to Chicago," she said.

He nodded once, then pushed his sunglasses onto the top of his tousled hair. The move revealed blue eyes that matched the sky above. And yeah. They were twinkling. Damn it.

"Understood. Just, uh, promise me you'll say 'Coffee, tea or me' at least once, okay? Please?"

Amanda tried to glare, but that twinkle sucked the annoyance right out of her. She could only draw in a slow breath as he climbed into the plane. As she watched her passenger disappear into the small jet, she had to wonder about the trip she was about to take.

Coffee and tea they had, and he was welcome to them. But her? Well, she'd never even considered making a move on a customer before. Talk about unprofessional.

And yet…

Something inside her suddenly wanted to take a chance, to be a little outrageous.

How long since she had done indecent things—or decent ones, for that matter—with a sexy man? Not since before they'd thrown all their energies into expanding Clear-Blue Air, at the very least. She hadn't had time for a lunch date, much less the kind of lust-fest she'd enjoyed in her younger years. The kind that lasted for entire weekends and involved not leaving a bed except to grab the kind of sensuous food that could be smeared onto—and eaten off—someone else's hot, naked, sweat-tinged body.

She closed her eyes, her hand clenching tight on the railing. Her heart fluttered in her chest and she tried to make herself move. But she couldn't—not climbing up, but not backing away, either. Not physically, and not in her head.

Was she really considering this? God, she hadn't even looked at the stranger's left hand to make sure he was available. She had no idea if he was actually attracted to her or just an irrepressible flirt. Yet something inside was telling her to take a shot with this man.

It was crazy. Something she'd never considered. Yet right now, at this moment, she was definitely considering it. If he was available…could she do it? Seduce a stranger. Have an anonymous fling, like something out of a blue movie on late-night cable?

She didn't know. All she knew was that the flight to Chicago was a short one so she had to decide quickly. And as she put her foot on the bottom step and began to climb up, Amanda suddenly had to wonder if she was about to embark on the ride of her life.

HARLEQUIN® *Blaze*™

It all started with a few naughty books....

As a member of the Red Tote Book Club, Carol Snow has been studying works of classic erotic literature…but Carol doesn't believe in love…or marriage. It's going to take another kind of classic—Charles Dickens's *A Christmas Carol*—and a little otherworldly persuasion to convince her to go after her own sexily ever after.

Cuddle up with

Her Sexy Valentine

by STEPHANIE BOND

Available February 2010

---

red-hot reads

www.eHarlequin.com

HB79526

REQUEST YOUR FREE BOOKS!

2 FREE NOVELS
PLUS 2
FREE GIFTS!

◆ HARLEQUIN®

INTRIGUE®

Breathtaking Romantic Suspense

YES! Please send me 2 FREE Harlequin Intrigue® novels and my 2 FREE gifts (gifts are worth about $10). After receiving them, if I don't wish to receive any more books, I can return the shipping statement marked "cancel." If I don't cancel, I will receive 6 brand-new novels every month and be billed just $4.24 per book in the U.S. or $4.99 per book in Canada. That's a saving of close to 15% off the cover price! It's quite a bargain! Shipping and handling is just 50¢ per book in the U.S. and 75¢ per book in Canada.* I understand that accepting the 2 free books and gifts places me under no obligation to buy anything. I can always return a shipment and cancel at any time. Even if I never buy another book from Harlequin, the two free books and gifts are mine to keep forever.

182 HDN E4EC   382 HDN E4EN

Name   (PLEASE PRINT)

Address   Apt. #

City   State/Prov.   Zip/Postal Code

Signature (if under 18, a parent or guardian must sign)

Mail to the **Harlequin Reader Service:**
IN U.S.A.: P.O. Box 1867, Buffalo, NY 14240-1867
IN CANADA: P.O. Box 609, Fort Erie, Ontario L2A 5X3
Not valid for current subscribers to Harlequin Intrigue books.

**Are you a subscriber to Harlequin Intrigue books and
want to receive the larger-print edition? Call 1-800-873-8635 today!**

* Terms and prices subject to change without notice. Prices do not include applicable taxes. N.Y. residents add applicable sales tax. Canadian residents will be charged applicable provincial taxes and GST. Offer not valid in Quebec. This offer is limited to one order per household. All orders subject to approval. Credit or debit balances in a customer's account(s) may be offset by any other outstanding balance owed by or to the customer. Please allow 4 to 6 weeks for delivery. Offer available while quantities last.

H1I0

HARLEQUIN *Presents*

PREGNANT BRIDES

Inexperienced and expecting,
they're forced to marry!

Bestselling Harlequin Presents author

Lynne Graham

brings you the second story
in this exciting new trilogy:

RUTHLESS MAGNATE, CONVENIENT WIFE

#2892

Available February 2010

Also look for

GREEK TYCOON, INEXPERIENCED MISTRESS

#2900

Available March 2010

www.eHarlequin.com

HP12892